CHEATED

Also by Patrick Jones

Things Change
Nailed
Chasing Tail Lights

CHEATED

Patrick Jones

WALKER & COMPANY
New York

To Brent

First published in the United States of America in 2008 by Walker Publishing Company, Inc.
Distributed to the trade by Macmillan

For information about permission to reproduce selections from this book, write to
Permissions, Walker & Company, 175 Fifth Avenue, New York, New York 10010

Library of Congress Cataloging-in-Publication Data
Jones, Patrick.
Cheated / Patrick Jones.
p.   cm.
Summary: Fifteen-year-old Mick recalls a series of betrayals and other life-changing events in his broken home, during the break-up with his girlfriend, and at school, that led to his arrest for murder.
ISBN-13: 978-0-8027-9699-8 • ISBN-10: 0-8027-9699-0
[1. Murder—Fiction. 2. Betrayal—Fiction. 3. Family problems—Fiction. 4. Interpersonal relations—Fiction. 5. High schools—Fiction. 6. Schools—Fiction. 7. Michigan—Fiction.]
I. Title.
PZ7.J7242Che 2008   [Fic]—dc22   2007018901

Visit Walker & Company's Web site at www.walkeryoungreaders.com

Book design by Nicole Gastonguay
Typeset by Westchester Book Composition
Printed in the U.S.A. by Quebecor World Fairfield
10 9 8 7 6 5 4 3 2 1

All papers used by Walker & Company are natural, recyclable products
made from wood grown in well-managed forests. The manufacturing processes
conform to the environmental regulations of the country of origin.

Acknowledgments

Thanks to Amy Alessio and Patricia Taylor, who read and made suggestions on early versions of *Cheated*. Also thanks to Laura Gajdostik, Kim Powers, and their students from Hudson (WI) High School for their continued support and input into my works in progress. Shout-out to Nick Campbell in Texas for all his inspiration. As always, thanks to Erica Klein for giving me the time and confidence to write fiction. Finally, a long overdue thank you slash acknowledgment to Emily Easton at Walker Books for Young Readers. I met Emily while serving on a committee selecting the best books for reluctant readers. Over a decade later, she helped me rewrite my first novel, which found a place on the very same list. While Things Change, Emily's support and guidance have remained constant.

Two roads diverged in a wood, and I—
I took the one less traveled by,
And that has made all the difference.
—Robert Frost, "The Road Not Taken"

Yes, there are two paths you can go by, but in the long run
There's still time to change the road you're on.
—Led Zeppelin, "Stairway to Heaven"

CHEATED

November 18, 9:00 a.m.

"It's really simple, kid," the investigator barks at me from across the table. He's trying to scare me. "The one who talks is the one who walks. So, I'll ask you the same thing I did when you came in here four days ago. What happened on November fifth?"

I'm trapped in an impossible situation. He's asking questions, but I've got no answers I can give—yet there's so much I want to say. My mind is a mess, littered with fear of the future, thoughts of the past, and one nagging question: how did my fifteen years of life lead me to staring death—in the form of a bloody dead body—in the face?

Part One
Friday, November 5

6:30 a.m.

I woke up that morning under dry sheets to the smell of coffee in my nose, the taste of cotton in my mouth, what felt like a brick smashing inside my skull, and a burning feeling in my gut. But not a single midnight memory of Nicole Snider resting in my brain. I was cheated even in my dreams that morning, never knowing, of course, that the day itself would end in a nightmare.

I turned off the buzzing alarm busting my eardrums, then buried my not-handsome-enough face into the soft pillow. I wanted to suffocate the thoughts of another day—although Fridays were the best day in my Nicole-less life. Friday was the day my best buds, Brody and Aaron, and I all told our moms we were going to the Swartz Creek High School football game. Instead, we'd hang at Aaron's sister's trailer drinking Bacardi 151, shooting the shit, and playing poker.

We'd started one night earlier than usual, at Aaron's suggestion, and I was paying the price. I crawled out of bed as if my feet contained all of my five ten, 160 pudgy pounds, and wanted to vomit. It made me wonder if it was called "hungover" because I'd spent the night with my head hung over the toilet trying to vomit. But here, too, I was a failure.

My stomach felt queasy, but worst was a headache aggravated by any noise, even the sound of the piss splashing into the water hurt my head. I reached into the medicine cabinet and pulled out a bottle of aspirin. I swallowed straight two round white clouds of relief and horded four for later in the day. When I brushed my teeth, I looked into the mirror and wondered what day I'd start shaving, what week the zits on my chin would disappear, and what month I'd look more like a man instead of this fifteen-year-old awkward mass of flesh, nerves, and want. I spat out disgust at myself with the toothpaste, then stumbled into the kitchen.

My mother was wrapped in an oversized white sweater and curled up on the kitchen floor sitting next to the heat vent, Kool in one hand, coffee in the other. Her bare face showed little signs of life, love, or the pursuit of happiness. I avoided her eyes, then looked through the faded yellow drapes at the frost-kissed leaf-covered backyard as she spoke. "Good morning, Mick."

I grunted, then grabbed milk from the fridge and poured a half glass. Maybe it was the distraction of my broken heart more than my throbbing head, but my hands didn't work, and I spilled milk on the counter. "Sorry," I said. I said that word a lot to everyone.

"Accidents happen," Mom said, as she moved from the floor, then walked toward me. She cleaned up my mess while I snatched the Rice Krispies box from the sparse cupboard. Except for buying fast food, neither shopping nor cooking were Mom's strengths. "Are you okay?"

I grunted, but I wanted to say, *No, Mom, I'm not okay and you're not okay, but let's keep lying to each other since the truth hurts.* I wanted to tell Mom a lot, but I couldn't say the words. I spent more time imagining conversations with her, and others, than I did having them.

"When did you get in?" she asked as I successfully poured milk into the cereal bowl.

"About ten," I mumbled. About ten after eleven was the truth, but I knew Mom had had a rare date after work, so she didn't get home until after midnight. My lie was safe, if unsound.

Mom sipped her coffee, then spoke. "Are you going to the game tonight?"

"I'm taking the booster bus with Brody and Aaron." I offered up the lie for her to challenge, but she let it go with a little half smile. She didn't like my friends, but didn't comment, unlike ex-Dad. He lectured me to "stay away from those who drag you down." I took ex-Dad's advice to heart and saw as little of him as possible.

"So, homecoming's next week," Mom said after an awkward quiet. My house seemed like a funeral home with all these long moments of silence. Even if I wanted to talk more to Mom, I couldn't because she was either working or too tired from working so many hours. She managed this snotty Chico's clothing store at Genesee Valley Mall. Outside the house, Mom always dressed in their private-label outfits, accessorized by her disappointed frown caused by her unkempt fashion-challenged son.

"I guess," I said in between swallows, but I wanted to say, *I know stupid homecoming is next week. You can't walk two feet at school without some prep or jock talking about it like it was the center of the universe.*

"Are you going to the homecoming dance?" Mom asked. I slurped down some milk, but wanted to say, *I had a chance to go with Nicole, but I screwed it up. I don't ask you about your boyfriends, so stay out of my love life, or lack thereof.*

"Probably," I mumbled my half-truth so she could only half hear it.

"You taking that Snider girl?" Mom doesn't know Nicole broke up with me on the first day of school; she doesn't know that I'm broken apart. The question was tentative; this was more of a conversation than we normally had. I wished there was a TV in the kitchen. I could have turned it on, and we could have watched other people talk to one another instead.

"No," I whispered as the cracking popping snapping cereal crashed into last evening's rum and Coke. I felt sick to my stomach, but sicker in my lonely boy circumstances.

Mom sighed, then spoke. "It's a little late to ask someone else out, don't you think?"

I rinsed out the bowl and the glass, but not the bad-tasting feeling that truth or lie, I was disappointing my mom either way. "I don't want to talk about it!" I shouted as I left the room.

"Fine," she snapped at me before she took a final drag and burned down the last hot embers on the Kool.

"Fine!" I shouted over my shoulder, but regretted that immediately. I wanted to say, *Mom, I'm sorry. You don't deserve this crap. I want to be a better son, but I don't know how.*

"One day you'll talk to me." Her words bounced in my

head, like a silver pinball at Space Invaders arcade. I wanted to turn around and admit my helplessness. *Mom, I want to talk to you so you can tell me what to do, but there's a wall and I just can't smash through it.*

Instead, I said nothing and retreated to my room, slamming the door behind me. I pulled cleaner clothes from the pile on the floor and got ready for school. I thought about wearing something other than my usual blue jeans and black T-shirt to impress Nicole, since she was now with that well-dressed college-bound bastard Kyle Miller. Yet I knew even if I changed my clothes, it wouldn't have made Nicole change her heart or her mind. I wanted to confess to her how I felt, how I deserved another chance, and how I wouldn't mess it up this time. But deep down, I knew I was lying to myself, as I often did. I can't even tell myself the truth, and admit it was all my fault. As I headed toward the shower that morning, I thought about turning the water on superhot. I wanted to burn away a layer of skin and scorch away my old self. I needed to become someone else; someone who wouldn't cheat or be cheated again. Nicole and I broke up because I was the one who cheated. How could I have known then that split-second decision would start me down a winding road filled with fire, smoke, and blood?

If you were looking at life in prison, then wouldn't you take a long look at your life?

Even if, like me, you've only lived life for fifteen years. My mom made me watch a movie once called Forrest Gump. *The guy in the movie keeps saying how life is like a box of chocolates, and you never know what you'll get. Even I know boxes of chocolates have those diagrams on the bottom that show you what's inside. No, life isn't like that at all. You want to know what life is like? You ever see a road map of the United States? That's life. It's a thousand possible roads, all of them somehow connected to each other. Some roads take you places where you can roll down the windows, let the music blast, and drive forever free; some roads lead you to places you thought you'd never be, like this place. There's one road out of this place and it's the road I cannot take. Instead, all I can do is open up the map in my head, run my finger backward from this place to the place before and the place before that, and think about the roads that got me here.*

7:00 a.m.

I blew off my mom's request that I wear a coat, so I stood on the curb in the cold waiting for the bus wrapped only in my black hoodie. I hated taking the bus, and couldn't wait until I turned sixteen when ex-Dad promised he'd buy me a car to drive to school. School's too far to walk to, and I'd rather die than have Mom haul my sorry ass, so I waited, alone. Sure, there was Whitney a few feet away, but she might as well be a thousand miles away. She was bundled up in a long brown winter coat with a bright yellow scarf and matching gloves and hat. When Whitney spoke in math class yesterday, I tried not to look at her. I tried to catch myself, thinking, *Stop staring*, but wanting Whitney—or most other girls—was like a wildfire, always changing directions.

Whitney stood with fellow preps Erin, Meghan, and Shelby, each one more beautiful and unreachable than the next. They laughed, baring their perfect white teeth to the gray fall sky. Their laughter was a cold hard rain falling down on me: it chilled, reduced, and angered me. I wanted to say to Whitney, *I'm not really a bad guy. I'm not smart enough or rich enough or good-looking enough for you, but I'd love only you.* I even took a step toward Whitney, but fear pushed me back. There's a brick wall of frustration firmly placed between the Whitney World and me. I felt like a doomed character in a Poe story: walled in, brick by brick; buried alive.

I never wanted to be a prep like Whitney or Kyle, nor a jock like Rusty Larson or Bob Fredericks, who strolled in all their three-letter cockiness toward the bus stop. Both of them jock jerk juniors who shouted at each other like they were on the football field. They yelled about nothing, other than to prove that this flat land was their mountain.

I clicked on my knockoff iPod (my jPod I call it) and felt the volume vibrating in my ears as I stared with silent rage at my fellow Swartz Creek Dragons. Music saved me and got me through that hate. Morning, noon, night, or whenever the Whitney World tempted me with unattainable beauty and the Rusty Bobs of school showed their colors of confidence, old Zeppelin, in particular "Stairway to Heaven," let me feel close to human. All the rage in my head and heart vanished into the volume of Plant's singing, Page's guitar, and the Jones-Bonham rhythm attack. I didn't need new music; the best music had already been recorded.

I blew on my ungloved hands; a cloud of white enveloped my paws. The cold didn't bother me as much as the wind crashing into my face, making my too-pink cheeks turn almost bloodred. When I stared at Whitney's bright, shiny smile and stylish new shoes, I felt more than ever like I no longer belonged in this neighborhood. In the divorce, Mom got the house, but little else. Ex-Dad left us surrounded by a nice life we see and seek every day, but can never again own.

I gazed down at my watch; some fancy model ex-Dad got me for my fifteenth birthday a few months ago. It was time to make a daily bet with myself on what would arrive

first: the yellow school bus or the long-brown-haired mountain known as Brody Warren. I saw the bus up the street just
as Brody rounded the corner, running on all pistons. I wondered if he was late because he wanted to be noticed making an entrance or to avoid ex-teammates Rusty and Bob.

"Dude," I said as I clicked off the music and came alive
for the first time that morning.

Brody slapped me on the back. Ash from his cigarette
sparked against the gray morning sky. "How you feelin', Mr.
151?" Brody asked as he offered me the smoke.

"Okay." I waved off the cigarette, but Brody pushed it
toward me.

"Better than ATM Aaron I bet," Brody said with a grin.
Like me, Brody was without a coat, any sense of fashion, or
access to a hairbrush. His long brown mane surrounded his
face, which was—unlike mine—sprouting a short jungle of
whiskers.

"No doubt," I told Brody, but my thoughts were with
Aaron. We called him "ATM" because he'd loaned us money
for the past three years. I wondered if last night we should've
said, *Aaron, what's with you? Why are you drinking so
much? Loan us some rum instead of cash.*

"Take it, dude," Brody insisted, and I took the cig. The
smoke tickled my mouth going in and burned my nose
coming out. I finished it, then threw the butt to the pavement. Brody's heavy boot ground it into the gray asphalt
like an ant that pissed him off. "You were so wasted last
night," he said in his volume-turned-up-to-ten voice.

"I guess," I replied, almost in a whisper. The Whitneys of

the world already thought I was a loser. They don't need to know they're right. Everybody already knew about Brody.

"Wasted!" Brody yelled to Rusty and Bob, who gathered up their backpacks adorned with the bloodred Swartz Creek Dragon logo. They were like twins and part of a family of forty brothers, all of them alike in their game day pressed khaki pants and Red Dragon jerseys. They sported football-season short hair and a complex look of pity, sadness, and disgust as they glared over at the fallen angel Brody. Their lips never moved but their eyes taunted, then rejected, Brody's existence. "Assholes," Brody mumbled as we fell last in line for the bus.

Nobody spoke when the bus pulled to the curb, a plume of exhaust briefly covering us all. Like lost explorers walking out of a jungle mist, we boarded the bus and took our unassigned but very much carved-in-stone seats. The Whitney World rode in the middle, while the Dragon True Believers sat up front like gatekeepers. We sank like stones in the back of the bus.

"Wasted," Brody hissed at Rusty and Bob when he passed by them. Big though they were, the jocks balled their fists but never moved their muscles against Brody, their ex-teammate. Brody was a varsity starter as a freshman; an all-state sure bet at training camp two months ago; a kicked-off-the-team loser who stood before them that football-Friday morning.

"Dude, let's go." But as soon as the words left my lips, I knew instead I should've said, *Dude, let* it *go*. I knew that was advice I should've given myself about so many things.

"Whatever, Pool Boy," Brody cracked, but I didn't laugh. I like Brody's 151 nickname for me better. This was a put-down name: I'm a terrible pool player, while Brody ruled the green felt. The pre-rum-filled run of the table the night before at Space Invaders arcade was the usual with Brody winning six games to my zero. Aaron won against me, lost against Brody, but didn't care either way. Brody's more athletic than me, while Aaron's hand-eye coordination is honed with hours of Xbox expertise. I suffered the humiliation as the price of friendship admission.

Our seat in the back was near the stoners like Dave Wilson. Dave's sleeping face was pressed against the window. If it were ten degrees colder, his drool would've frozen on his chin.

"What time?" Brody asked as he pushed himself into the seat and tossed his backpack onto my lap. It didn't hurt since the nearly empty pack weighed so little. I took a few college prep courses, but Brody's college future vanished with his football banishment. He'd given up even caring about school.

I was puzzled by the question: what time for what? What time was it? What time would we get together later that night? I was still thinking when Brody grabbed my wrist.

"Nice watch." Brody grunted, then kicked the seat in front of him. "Your dad, right?"

"Yeah, ex-Dad," I corrected him as his eyes closed. I should've said, *Brody, your dad left your life because of an accident on the road. My dad's exit was no accident; it was because of the road I decided to take.*

While Brody slept, I put the headphones back on, then clicked on the jPod to drown out the noise surrounding me. I was lost in crashing music and imaginary conversations as the bus made one of its last stops. The stop was in front of the WindGate trailer park, where Roxanne Gray slithered on board. She wore a denim jacket with a white skull patch, a tan wool cap that pushed her brown hair out like the top of a chocolate muffin, and her usual crooked half smile. I ignored her that morning like I had done most every day for years; like I wished I'd done weeks ago at Rex's end-of-summer, life-ruining party. I wanted to ask her, *Roxanne, why did you choose me to fool around with? Why didn't you pick somebody else?* Instead, I listened to Zeppelin and stayed mute until the jolt of the bus stopping woke up Brody.

He coughed loudly, then looked outside as the bus lurched down Morrish Road toward school. "I wonder if the Scarecrow is out there yet?" Brody asked, then closed his eyes again.

"Too early, probably sleeping it off," I replied. "Like I wish I could've done."

"Well, you ain't no Scarecrow," Brody said, then bounced his beefy paw off my knee.

"Guess not," I offered, then looked near the entrance ramp to the expressway for the Scarecrow, a homeless guy with long, dirty blond hair, ratty clothes, and a straw hat, which was why Brody called him the Scarecrow. He held up a sign that said HUNGRY VET, PLEASE HELP, GOD BLESS, but few cars stopped. One day ex-Dad stopped, rolled down the window, and yelled at him, "Get a job," then drove away. I heard his reply. If ex-Dad did, he never reacted when the Scarecrow yelled back, "Where?" I'd seen the Scarecrow by the road other times and by the Big K Market.

The last part of the ride was as silent for Brody and me as it was noisy for the rest of the bus. The noise swirled with the force of a hurricane, but I acted calm as the bus pulled into the school's circular driveway. Whitney World and the Dragon True Believers seemingly sprang from the bus and rushed toward school, while the stoners, the waking wild man Brody, and I stumbled like zombies from the grave toward the building's front door.

Do you know what it's like to be paralyzed?

That's how I felt: I couldn't make my mouth open or my tongue move. All I could do was listen and watch. Listen to the sick sound of a brick smashing against a human skull, then watch the blood splatter like red rain. From across the few feet that separated me from the very real scene before me, I could hear the smack of brick against bone. It sounded like someone dropping a heavy book off a desk. My eyes were wide, gazing at his eyes, open to the world and closed off to life. My nose cut through the rancid smells already in the air and the rancid mess he made in his pants as life left him. Another hard smash of the brick right above those lifeless eyes left me with the image I'll never erase: his left eye swollen shut, the right one wide open, staring, it seemed, right into my soul. He was a nonliving answer to a question I had never asked: what did a dead body look like?

8:00 a.m., Homeroom

I headed straight for my locker, wondering if my lockermate, Aaron, would be there. I was supposed to share a locker with my ex-friend Garrett, but after this summer, those plans changed. Brody still had to share with Ben Rankin, one of his ex-teammates, so his locker was covered with Spirit Club streamers and balloons. I walked head down through halls ringing with wild laughter, flowing red crepe paper, and the sounds of happy couples laughing.

My locker was bare. Aaron's army surplus jacket sat on top of a stack of his magazines with video game cheat codes. I was surprised to see Aaron's stuff after last night's mix of rum, cola, and unexpected angry mood. I dropped off some books, so by the time I stepped through the doorway of Mr. Steinbach's noisy homeroom, the bell had gone silent.

"Please be quiet for announcements," Steinbach said to little reaction.

I put my head down on my desk, closed my eyes, and made up my own announcements rather than listen to the endless list of clubs, events, and activities that touched my life not at all: *May I have your attention, please? Mick Salisbury would like to announce that he's sorry about what he did to Nicole, he wants her back, and he wants her to know it wasn't his fault. Mick also wants to announce that Roxanne Gray is a lying slut. Everybody have a great Dragon Day!*

I loved homeroom last year; that's where I'd met Nicole. By the ninth day of ninth grade, I'd fallen for her. I remember how her long brown hair always fell in her face. I would see her in homeroom and long to reach over, brush it back, and see her brown eyes smile at me.

I got her attention last year by doing fake announcements: *Your attention, please! The Chess Club challenges the Mathletes to a geek-off. The horn section of the Marching Band would like to tell the school: blow us. If you've ever wanted to see France, join the French Club. If you'd prefer to see Jackson State Prison, then please join Dave Wilson and the stoners after school behind the bleachers. Finally, for all seniors wanting to graduate this year, the teachers would like to say "Good riddance, you losers." Now, have a great Dragon Day!* She'd laugh, even at the weaker, unfunny ones. What she was really laughing at, I thought, was how hard I was trying to impress her and make her like me.

The only girl in this year's homeroom that interested me above the belt was the one Brody called Cell Phone Girl. Even though we had two classes together last year and homeroom this year, I still didn't even know her name. That fact said something, even if she never ever did. While I'm not one to volunteer to speak, I'd talk in class if the teacher called on me. But this girl never said a word to anyone, not teacher or student. The teachers rarely said anything to her, other than to tell her to put away her cell phone, which she never did for long. She used no makeup, had dirty blond hair that was either greasy or unwashed, and wore an oversized gray hooded sweatshirt. She'd put her head down on her desk, when Steinbach wasn't looking, but somehow I could always see her peek at the phone buried in the sweatshirt's pocket. Her best move was to transfer the cell phone from the pocket and bury it in the sleeve. She'd pull down the sleeve or nudge the phone out every five minutes or so, look all sad again, and then put her head back down on the desk. As isolated as I felt, especially after Nicole dumped me, I couldn't imagine what was going on with Cell Phone Girl. I wanted to say to her, *Tell me what's wrong and I'll help.*

That morning, I was obsessed with wondering if people wondered about me. Were other people in homeroom thinking of things they'd like to say to me? Was Cell Phone Girl sitting there, in between phone peeks and sullen sighs, thinking, I wonder what's going on with Mick Salisbury? He's dating Nicole, and he loses her for a couple of seconds with Roxanne? What's wrong with him? Oh, right, his dad was like that, too. But Cell Phone Girl never spoke to me, and I never tried to know her. We sat just feet apart, but with miles between us.

By the time the bell rang for first period, I'd asked myself that same question: what *was* wrong with me? I knew that home was where the heart was broken. Always hovering over my life was how ex-Dad betrayed my mom, then I betrayed him. But two wrongs didn't make anything right. The base of this triangle of lies was ex-Dad's refusal to confess or repent. His brick wall of silence, of refusing to admit responsibility, stuck like a bone in my throat. Mom used to talk about it more, especially when she was in therapy after the divorce. She always said that until ex-Dad accepted responsibility, then none of us would be fully healed. I didn't much care about ex-Dad's healing, I cared more about hearing his apology or explanation.

As I trudged slowly from homeroom out into the hall-way, I thought not about school but about home. Thinking about Mom and ex-Dad made me walk slower, like a pile of bricks was on my back. Your family isn't just your family: it is your history, your future, and your burden.

Do you think about being famous?

Everybody I know does. Most won't come right out and talk about it, but it's always there underneath the surface. That's why I used to do those mock interviews with Brody. It made him feel like a star. But not just Brody; anybody who ever picked up a football, baseball, or basketball thinks one day they're going to end up on ESPN, on the cover of Sports Illustrated, *or at the least in the local newspaper, the* Flint Journal. *Anybody who's ever sung a note, or played in the band, or acted, must think about cutting a CD, making a music video, or starring in a movie. I never did any of those things—I'm not a jock or some band geek— but that doesn't mean I didn't have dreams of being famous. Now I would dread seeing my name in the paper. I wouldn't be famous, but infamous. But I don't have to worry about reading the paper myself because they don't let you do that at the Genesee County Juvenile Detention Center.*

First Period

I hated whoever made up my school schedule, putting Project Physics first hour. Project Physics was one of the many code words at Creek for "no-college kids." I knew that Whitney and her group were two doors down in real physics, while Nicole and a select few took honors physics. Their futures burned bright, while I toiled away in darkness.

The worst part of first period was my second glimpse of Roxanne. She sat on the other side of the room, so short that I could barely see her on the stool. She wore black mascara, dark brown lipstick, and two big silver hoop earrings. Her tight black Snoop Dogg T-shirt showed off her stomach, and her eyes showered me in shame. I paid little attention to Mr. Gates as he rambled on about the project before us, because I couldn't get my mind off the past or my eyes off Roxanne. I laughed when Mr. Gates reminded us not to put our hands in the fire when we used the Bunsen burners. I glared at Roxanne and knew it was a "been there, done that" moment.

It was at a pool party at Rex Wallace's house over Labor Day. The partygoers were mainly football players, and they'd all signed Words of Honor, a pledge not to drink or do drugs. They were mostly older kids, but since Brody made varsity as a tenth-grader, he was invited. And where Brody went, I followed. Aaron was busy with his mom and stepdad, while Nicole and her family were camping in Canada.

She'd only be gone a few days but I missed her badly, and for once couldn't wait for school to start so I could see her every day. Brody kept pushing me for details about Nicole as we walked over to the party, but I stayed quiet since I didn't have much to tell. I desperately loved Nicole, but she wouldn't let me show it beyond kissing. At the party, Brody was thirsty and I was hungry for Nicole. With an empty stomach and a troubled mind I created the chemical compound that exploded my life.

Brody had lifted a bottle of rum from Rex's parent's liquor cabinet, and the two of us took off, which was fine since I didn't know many people at the party anyway. We went into the woods behind Rex's house only to find Roxanne and other WindGate girls getting high. Even though Brody and I barely knew them, they invited us to party with them. Brody declined, but dared me to partake. When Roxanne passed me the joint, her tiny fingers set off odd reactions in me. I wanted to ask Roxanne: *Why are you here? You're not a prep or a cheerleader. You're not dating a football player. You're in with the wrong crowd, like me.*

After a while, the other girls and Brody headed back to the party, while Roxanne and I stayed behind. She took off her jacket, put it down on the brown dirt and patches of grass, then lowered herself onto it. I took one look at Roxanne's wet inviting mouth and knew I should run away. Instead, I let her pull me down and lay on the cold ground next to her. But the cold earth didn't sober me up. Mom had beaten me up since day one about drugs, yet I'd betrayed her because it was so easy and available. All those endless lectures, all those DARE classes at school, and now all those words meant nothing.

I looked into Roxanne's mascara-heavy eyes, then glanced back toward the party. I thought about those confident football players, and I knew I didn't belong. I didn't even deserve to be with Nicole, she was too good for me. No, I really belonged with the other losers, like Roxanne. She pushed up against me and whispered something into my ear about scoring. As we kissed, she held on to me, but not around the shoulders; she put her hands on my belt. Her tongue tickled my ear while her fingers unbuckled my belt. The summer breeze washed over my face as Roxanne pushed my pants down just far enough. My feet remained perfectly still and my left arm wrapped around Roxanne; my right arm was useless as Roxanne's tiny hand took control. For that second, our eyes met, but no words were exchanged. It was just Roxanne's crooked smile and my heavy breathing. When it was over, I pulled up my pants but remained on the cold ground stunned as if I'd been struck by skin-burning lightning.

In Project Physics that morning, thinking about the past, I was angry at Roxanne for stumbling into my path. But she wasn't the only target of my anger. I hated whatever person told Nicole, but the heat didn't belong there either. I guess I hated Brody for putting the rum in my hand and the evening in motion. Even through smudged safety glasses, I could see that the red-hot fury really belonged in one place and one place alone. I ignored Mr. Gates shouting out my name as I put my hand over the small Bunsen burner, giving my pain badly needed, if only temporary, release.

Did you know that not all blood is red?

On TV, it looks crimson, like our school colors. Bright. Vivid. Or maybe that's just the color of blood from the living, not from the dead. We checked his pulse and there was none, so the heart didn't pump the blood, it just oozed out of him. Gravity took over as the almost purple liquid dripped out of the deep wounds in the dead body drop by drop. We were there when he made the transition from person to corpse. The blood mixed with the brown dirt and the yellow and red leaves, like a box of dark-colored Crayolas melting in the sun. That must be the color of a rainbow in hell.

Second Period

My quick trip to the school nurse and around the truth of my not-so-accidental accident made me late for math, which was my best subject. I handed the pass to Mrs. Webster hoping she wouldn't notice the bandage on my hand, and walked to my seat slowly, trying in vain to make eye contact with Whitney. But the numbers on the board were more important to her than my sad smile. I wanted to stop at her desk and whisper, *Whitney, please save me from myself.* Instead, I went straight to my seat next to Aaron. Aaron shot me a half smile, readjusted his glasses, then tugged on his blond hair as he focused his bloodshot eyes on the blackboard.

Up on the board, Mrs. Webster was drawing various triangles. I didn't need math to see three-sided shapes: me, Brody, and Aaron; me, Mom, and ex-Dad. Only the girls I thought about had more than three sides—from Whitney, who I lusted after, to Nicole, who I yearned for; from Roxanne, who I was angry at, to Cell Phone Girl, who I was curious about. Girls in my world weren't a triangle, a circle, or a square; they were an infinite plane. But everywhere else, I saw triangles. Go to church and talk about the Trinity. Study government and learn about the three branches. There might be two sides to every story, but it took three sides to make that story interesting.

Of them all, it was the triangle of Brody, Aaron, and me that was strongest. We shared more than poker, jokes, and rum; we were all abandoned sons. One of the first things Brody and I learned about Aaron was how he almost died in the same car accident that took his father's life. Brody and Aaron miss the joy of having their dads around. Even if ex-Dad only saw me every other weekend, he took full advantage of that time by bossing me around and telling me how to behave, to stay away from Brody, and to teach me life lessons, like how to be smart with money.

Ex-Dad has this crazy thing about money. He's a fanatic about always counting the change and keeping the books. When I visit him, he lets me earn money doing chores around the apartment, but then he brings out "the book." The book is a small black accounting ledger and part of the deal. Ex-Dad pays me for my work, but I need to record the money I get and show him, down to the last penny and including receipts, how I spend it. When I was younger, it was easy to do since I'd spend my money on stuff ex-Dad approved of. By high school, I had to make up lies and get money from Aaron to buy stuff "off the book." I'd learned in social studies how big companies did stuff like that all the time, cheating people out of millions of dollars by faking their own books, so it didn't seem like such a big deal.

I tried to concentrate on the problems on the board, but Whitney's perfect shape was only three desks away. I couldn't see her face, just the blond hair stretching down her back. I imagined that hair swaying to music, the music of the homecoming dance. I could imagine the whole scene now. I'd have Mom drive us to the dance; I would see the pride in her eyes as she said, "*Whitney, a pleasure to meet you.* But more than that, I could imagine Nicole coming up to me during the dance, saying, *Mick, I forgive you; let's get back together.*

"Aaron, I need a favor," I whispered as I tapped my pencil against his desk.

"Name it," Aaron replied. His attention wasn't on me or the blackboard but on the *Electronic Gaming Monthly* magazine stuffed inside his math book.

"Can you loan me sixty bucks?" I asked, half ashamed, half anxious with anticipation. I was talking to Aaron, but staring at Whitney. Even when her best friend, Shelby, caught me staring and shot me a dirty look, I still couldn't look away from Whitney.

"Sure," Aaron answered, as he always did. Brody and I liked Aaron, and welcomed him in as our friend, but the truth was, he also bought his way in. Aaron's new stepdad used money as buddy barter; it seemed to be a lesson Aaron practiced himself.

"Thanks, I owe you," I said out of habit since I never paid him back in cash.

"What's wrong with your hand?" Aaron asked, as his fingers nervously twisted his longish blond hair. I'd seen Aaron pull out long strands by accident. "You get in another fight?"

I laughed, but managed to avoid capture by Mrs. Webster's glare. "No, an accident."

"What's it for?" Aaron asked as he reached for his wallet. "Just curious, doesn't matter."

"Homecoming tickets for me and Whitney," I whispered as I waited for three twenties.

"Whitney?" Aaron knew all about my lust life, but he rarely reciprocated by sharing details with Brody and me about his long-distance girlfriend, Debbie. "You're not getting back with Nicole?"

"Nicole's dead to me," I said overdramatically, like I was trying to convince myself.

"We'll drink to another death then," Aaron said with a wink, then turned to face Mrs. Webster after handing me the bills. She was discussing a proof, but all I could think about was the proof of the rum we'd drink later that night.

Have you ever been drunk?

It sounds better than it feels. The big thing in junior high was to brag about getting drunk. It was like a badge of honor not only to get drunk but to make sure everybody knew about it. I noticed most people told stories about getting drunk with cousins at parties, or while camping, all stories that were probably just lies. You do that a lot in junior high, lie about stupid small stuff, lie to impress people, lie to escape punishment from your parents. And lie just because you can. I never lied to Mom about being drunk, because she never asked, and she never noticed. Except for a few times here and there, it wasn't something Brody and I did a lot, maybe because his father was a drunk. Aaron was the one who kind of pushed us to do it with him, which was funny because he normally did what we wanted. But freshman year he told us that his sister would buy booze for us, if we gave her some money, and we could use her trailer to drink. We tried beer, Jack Daniels, lots of stuff. But Brody was the big one for Bacardi, so in tenth grade that was all we drank. Unlike other people, though, we didn't brag about it outside of our circle. It was our secret, but as Brody and I found out that night, it wasn't the only secret that Aaron was keeping. Keeping secrets is a lot like getting drunk: it makes you feel good at first, but in the long run, it just eats away at your life.

Third Period

I bolted out of my seat at the back of the room and got to the door in record time as the second period bell rang, but I couldn't get the words out of my mouth. When Whitney walked past me, her books cradled where I longed to put my head, I couldn't say, *Whitney, would you come to homecoming with me?* My tongue tied up in my mouth, and sweat rolled down my forehead in the overheated hall. Unable to speak in English, I took a deep breath, and hurried to Spanish.

Ten minutes into the class, my head was down on the desk, one ear open in case Mr. Rice called on me, one eye open on ex-friend Garrett in case he finally wanted to settle his debt.

It all went down, the fight and our friendship, a few days after the end of our freshman year. We were out back behind Garrett's house. Brody had Aaron gather some kindling, while Garrett and I dug a pit. It took just one flick from Brody's bone white lighter to start the fire. Everybody was in a bad mood because Aaron didn't get us anything to drink. I was surprised to even be there since I'd noticed a change in Garrett. While we all went our separate ways after school—Brody to sports, Aaron to his Xbox, Garrett to student council stuff, and me to my house to watch TV or listen to music—we'd remained tight. But by the end of the year, Garrett started dressing nicer, talking a little less trash, and hanging out with us a lot less. So, it was cool that Garrett wanted to hang with us again.

We started talking about the only thing that mattered: girls at school. Garrett started the conversation and suggested we name names of different girls at school who we'd want to hook-up with. Brody jumped right in and went first. He surprised us by naming Cell Phone Girl. I guessed Brody wanted to figure her out as much as I do. Aaron went next, naming Debbie, the never-seen girlfriend from Detroit. But we pressed him to name someone that the rest of us knew, so he offered up the name of Terri White, who was Nicole's best friend.

It came to my turn, but before I could even answer, all three shouted Nicole's name. They enjoyed watching my face turn scarlet in embarrassment, but saw it change to red-hot anger when Garrett said, "If Nicole was my girl-friend, I'd do it with her until my dick fell off."

"Well, at least I have a girlfriend," I shouted at Garrett. He didn't need to know Nicole and I hadn't done anything, nor ever would, thanks to her "purity pledge."

"My turn. You know who I'd love to do," Garrett said, then pointed at me like he was calling me out. "Your mom. I tell you, Mick, she's one hot MILF!"

"Dude, that's so wrong," Aaron said, breaking his normal code of silence.

"What, it's true, isn't it?" Garrett shouted at Aaron, but he was looking at me.

"Shut up," Brody shouted.

I was angry, yet strangely paralyzed, unable to move in defense of my mom. When Garrett started laughing, I dove into him, and we rolled through the remains of the fire. I threw punches, and at first, Garrett covered up and kept laughing. The smack of my hand against his head was ineffective, and he rolled on top of me. I got my hands up, but Garrett was quick with a punch, splitting open my eyebrow. The sound of Garrett's fists bouncing off my skull crackled like crossed wires. Sweat mixed with blood flowed down my face like a raging river. But before Garrett could land the knockout punch, Brody ended the fight, with a hard stiff kick to Garrett's face. Garrett went down flat on his back like he'd been hit with a ton of bricks. "Let's go," was all Brody said, as I pulled myself off the ground, dusted the black ash from my shirt, and wiped the blood from my face. Aaron quickly followed Brody, and the three of us left Garrett's big mouth and probably broken nose behind.

Garrett and I never spoke again, exchanging only angry looks at school. Like ex-Dad, he wouldn't admit fault or say he was sorry. When Mom asked why I wasn't friends with Garrett, I just grunted, but I wanted to say, *I don't see Garrett anymore because Garrett said he wanted to fuck you. I stood up for you again. I've stood up for you twice, so when will you protect me?*

My eyes were closed as memories flooded my mind until I heard Mr. Rice say almost into my ear, "*Tiene bueno siesta Señor Salisbury?*"

"Mucho bueno." I picked my heavy head up off the desk, waited until Mr. Rice turned around, and then swallowed down two more aspirin. In a few hours, my head would stop hurting from drinking too much, and in a few weeks my heart might stop hurting from missing Nicole. But as I looked at my bandaged hand, I wondered when my life would be healed.

What was the worst day of your life?

Before November 5, it was June 18. That's the day that I destroyed my family. It was just a few days after school was out; I'd just finished fifth grade. Brody's mother took him, his two brothers, and me to the mall. Brody's brothers went one way, we went another. What if we would have gone with them to the food court instead of the arcade? What if we would have been there an hour earlier or an hour later? What if I wouldn't have seen my father and a woman who was not my mom come out of a jewelry store laughing, kissing, and holding hands?

"Buddy, let me explain." Dad rushed over like he was putting out a fire.

"Daddy, who is she?" At ten, I didn't understand all the rules of the adult world, but I knew this woman wasn't my mother and that my father shouldn't be kissing her.

"Mick, listen, she's an old friend of mine," he'd said. "It's not what you think, buddy."

"But you were—" I started, not really knowing the right words to capture what I saw, not knowing what I should feel, only knowing my father wasn't telling me the truth.

"Your mother doesn't need to know about this, you understand," he'd said, then put his hand gently on my shoulder. "You have to promise not to tell her about this, buddy."

"But—" I stopped when Dad's gentle touch turned to a hard squeeze.

"Mick, look, I'll explain all this later," my father said, but

I knew that was a lie, too. "Do I have your word? Your word, Mick, is your bond. I can trust you, right, buddy?"

If I promised my dad, I let him betray Mom. If I told Mom, I was betraying him. My hands stayed by my sides, my eyes on the floor, and I walked away unsure what to think, feel, or do. If you were me, what would you have done?

Fourth Period

I hated PE, but it was the only class in the day where I saw Brody, although he was late as usual. I guessed he was in the principal's office. Since he was no longer on the football team, Brody caught crap from everyone for everything. I tried to make a quick change in the locker room, but Rex Wallace cornered me.

"What's up, 151?" Rex said to me, then smacked my arm.

"Why do you call him 151?" some stupid jock standing behind Rex asked.

"It's because I'm so smart; it's my IQ," I said.

"No, it's because he's a drunk like Brody," Rex replied, his voice loaded with contempt.

"Whatever," I said.

"Bob and Rusty told me they caught you staring at Whitney at the bus stop," Rex said, his voice all puffed up like his chest. "Don't even think about it."

"Think about what?"

"You already blew it with Nicole, but anybody could have seen that coming," Rex continued, pushing his finger into my face. "Face it, loser, you're out of your league."

I wanted to tell him, *I know that, Rex, but I'm trying real hard to forget it.*

"Just let Roxanne do you again," he said as he smacked my arm.

Before I could respond, I heard Brody's thundering voice. "Knock if off, Rex!"

"Relax, Brody," Rex said, then turned to face him.

"Don't tell me what to do," Brody said, then spat at Rex's feet.

"You have no discipline," Rex shouted. "You cost us a state championship."

"And you have no dick," Brody shouted back. "And no balls!"

"Take it back," Rex said.

"You take back what you said about me," Brody shouted as he took one step closer.

"What do you mean?" Rex said, taking one step back.

"I know it was you," Brody said as he tilted his head to the left. He looked a little crazy.

"What are you talking about?"

"You turned me in, you ratted me out." Brody jabbed his finger hard into Rex's chest.

Rex took another step back. "Don't blame me for something that's your own fault."

"That's not the point," Brody said. "You don't rat out your friends."

Rex tempted fate and facial injuries by letting out a small laugh as he said, "Brody, you were my teammate, you were never my friend."

Brody responded not by shouting, but by whispering, "If it was you, I'll kill you."

Rex staggered back, just as Coach Simpson arrived. He was wearing a baseball cap to cover his bald head and a windbreaker to hide his gut. "What's going on here?" Simpson said.

Rex looked at Brody, and then at the floor before he said, "Nothing, Coach."

"Very well, then. Let's pump some iron," Coach Simpson said as he unlocked the weight room door with one of the fifty keys on his chain. Turning that key was the highlight of his teaching efforts for the day.

Like a leper, Brody walked by other ex-teammates to hit the bench press. Like everybody else on the football team, he had signed the Words of Honor oath not to drink or do drugs. He kept to it freshman year. He'd been a killer on the field, moved up from JV to varsity after three games. He was a running-back vacuum consuming any ball carrier that came his way. The team lost in the state semis, but Brody was a tackling machine in the tournament game.

At the Labor Day party, Brody started the night in the basement shooting pool. He won game after game. Pretty soon, no one would play him, so I took on the tackling dummy task. After a while two senior teammates wanted the table. Brody told them to go to hell, but they pushed him away. Rex walked over and told Brody it was his house, his table, and his rules. I whispered to Brody it was time to go. He gave up the pool table but kept his cue. He let out a string of curses as he stomped to the other end of the basement. He looked at the locked glass liquor cabinet, then yelled across the crowded, noisy room at Rex. "Where's the key?"

"The key to what?" Rex shouted back, but it was too late.

Brody took the pool cue like a baseball bat and shattered the glass of the Wallaces' liquor cabinet. He reached in so fast to grab the Bacardi bottle that he didn't seem to notice the glass cutting his arm.

"Brody, you asshole," Rex shouted as he, and a few others, headed toward Brody.

"I know, your house, your rules," Brody shouted back, then with a mostly full bottle of Bacardi, we raced up the stairs, past the pool, and out into the woods. Less than an hour later, after I ruined my life with Roxanne, we were both back downstairs. Since no one could beat him at pool, he loudly challenged his fellow teammates to any other contest.

"Go home, Brody," Rex said, realizing Brody wasn't leaving on his own.

"Make me," Brody shouted back.

"Guys, help me out here," Rex said, and finally there was strength in numbers as three or four soft-drink-breathing Dragons stalked toward Brody. Before they could lay a hand on him, Brody made a break, tearing up the stairs and out the front door this time. I was one step behind him. He headed for the street and jumped on the hood of a Grand Am parked in front of Rex's house. He then leaped from car roof to car roof, leaving in his wake the smell of rum and the loud ringing of alarms that sounded like a tornado warning siren blaring into the night.

Brody kicked me back into the present when he said, "Hey, 151, I need a little payback."

"What's up?" I replied.

"Your dick whenever Whitney's in the room."

"Serious."

"Think you could help me out over lunch? I need help typing up Kirby's stupid English paper," Brody said as I added a few more pounds for his next lift. "I'll owe you."

I nodded my agreement, but wondered why Brody had said, "I'll owe you." I wanted to reply, *Brody, we're friends, we don't owe each other anything other than friendship. You, me, and Aaron, that's all that matters: not his money, your muscle, and whatever it is you guys see in me.* But I didn't say anything; I just kept it all inside. As he pumped iron, I felt my frustration, with Rex, with Nicole, but mostly with myself, pump like poison through my veins.

Do you remember when you met your best friend?

I was five, almost six, riding my bike just up and down the driveway; I wasn't allowed by Mom to go out into the street. I'd seen a kid who looked about my age now at the end of the driveway. It was a beautiful fall day, but my mom made me wear this ugly orange windbreaker to protect me from the cold. Brody pulled his bike into the driveway; he was wearing a big smile and a Lions T-shirt. Even then his hair was long, and he was bigger than most kids our age.

"Hey, you wanna ride bikes?" Brody shouted, still at the end of the driveway.

"Um, I'm not supposed to go out of the driveway," I replied.

"What's your name?" he called out, then added, "I'm Brody."

"Michael," I said softly because even then I hated my name. "Call me Mick."

"Mick, come on, just down the street. I'll race you," Brody said then inched closer.

"I'm not supposed to be in the street. Mom said," I replied, so embarrassed.

"Dare you, double dare you," Brody put his bike next to mine. He pretended the bike's handlebars were a motorcycle, making loud sounds as his hands rubbed the bars. "Let's go!"

I paused for a second as Brody took off with me in pursuit. I rode that day until my bottom was sore. It was more sore later when Mom found out and my dad spanked me

CHEATED

until I think I heard a bone crack in his hand. I couldn't have known then, of course, that if I hadn't followed Brody down the road that day, my life would be so different now, and forever.

Lunch

I hightailed it from gym, not even showering—which was my usual routine—so I could stake out a computer in the school library. I easily got around the filter, the way Aaron had showed me, and checked my messages. But there was nothing from Nicole, to no surprise yet bitter disappointment. The only person I knew in the library was Cell Phone Girl. She was by herself in the corner pretending to read a magazine while text messaging on her phone.

I kept looking at the clock in the library willing it to move faster, to bring Brody, but once again, I felt helpless. That's one of the worst things about waiting: that feeling of helplessness. Like counting the change, my Salisbury DNA imprinted a hatred of waiting. Ex-Dad won't go to a drive-through fast-food window if there's more than two cars in front of him. He would walk out on promised outings, like movies or baseball games, before standing in any line.

But I waited. It was all I did anymore. Not just wait for Brody, but for Nicole to talk to me again, and take me back. Some of the worst waiting were the hours between when I cheated on Nicole and when she found out. Maybe it was how guys in prison on death row feel.

And if not Nicole, then I waited for Whitney, or someone like her, to love me. I waited for Roxanne to say she was sorry she'd messed things up with Nicole. I waited for Nicole to forgive me for messing up, and for me to forgive myself.

I know Mom's never forgiven ex-Dad. I waited for him to apologize for his broken promises, his lies, and for making me choose. As I stared at the clock, all I could remember was after the divorce waiting in offices for lawyers and counselors. It didn't matter if it was good waiting or bad waiting, all of it left me with the same feelings of helplessness and burning anger. Once the fire starts, it doesn't care what's in its path; it doesn't choose, it just consumes.

With less than fifteen minutes left in the lunch period and my stomach not just growling but screaming, Brody finally showed up so I could type up his report on the poem "The Road Not Taken" by Robert Frost, for Mrs. Kirby's English class, which he had next period.

"So, where are your notes?" I asked him.

He just smiled as he opened up a black notebook. At the top of the page it said "The Road Not Taken" and at the bottom it said Brody Warren. And there was nothing in between.

"You didn't write anything?" I said, so frustrated.

"Well, we were busy last night, 151," Brody said, then laughed too loud for a library. I wanted to say, *Brody, we've had two weeks to do this paper, why did you wait until the last minute?* But that's not the thing you say to a friend unless you're turning into your mom.

As I thought about what to say next, I imagined those scenes in cartoons where the character had the devil on one shoulder and an angel on the other. Sometimes I wished I could perform brain surgery on myself and cut out the part known as the conscience. Instead, I would just numb the nerves that Friday night with the only sedatives available.

"Mick, dude, help a friend out," Brody pushed. "Like I said, I'll owe you."

I knew I'd never figure out the balance sheet between Brody and me. I did stuff like this for Brody all the time, but Brody, like the thing with Rex, certainly did things for me. I opened up a blank Word document and typed in the title and Brody's name.

"How do you know stuff?" Brody asked me.

"What do you mean?" I responded.

"Like what to write about some poem. I don't get it," Brody says, his voice a mix of admiration for me, confusion at the world, and frustration with himself for his limitations.

"I don't know, I just do," I said, but I wanted to say, *I'll tell you if you tell me how to be like you: strong and fearless.* But instead I started typing my words under his name.

Brody gave me a good-natured slap on the back as he got up to leave. "Dude, I'll save you a seat in the 'teria." As Brody walked through the library, he looked like he owned it.

"Thanks," I said, to myself, typing away as Brody left me behind. I don't blame Brody for who he is. He grew up with two older brothers, both of them a lot bigger than him. I remember big tough Brody crying like a girl after one of his brothers would kick his ass. His mother was useless, and his father mostly absent. After his dad died, things got worse for a few years. But once Brody's oldest brother, Jack, graduated from high school, he signed up for the army. Cooper graduated the next year and followed—as he did in all things—in Jack's footsteps, but never made it out of basic training. He was serving—not overseas, but ten years in a military prison for beating up an officer.

As I stared at the blank Word document, the blazing white screen was a light illuminating my mind. Frost was wrong: it's the roads we *take*, like following Brody on my bike that day, that make all the difference.

Don't you wish your life had an undo button like Microsoft Word?

When you mess up, and you know you've messed up, you could just press a button, and whatever you did wrong would be undone. Then click it again and undo the thing that led you to mess up. Then again, and again, until you return yourself to an innocent baby. You know why babies are innocent? Not because they don't do bad things, but because they don't know bad from good so they can't make a choice. All my life, I thought I wanted to be able to make my own decisions, never realizing choices don't make you free; they tie you down.

Fifth Period

I stumbled into history hungry for food and desperate for sleep. Writing Brody's paper took longer than I thought it would, so lunch wasn't my usual pile of fries and pizza slices but a can of Coke and my last two aspirin instead. I was in no mood to hear about the problems of the Greeks or listen to the geeks in the class kiss up to Mr. Lomax. It seems to me that history is simple. I wanted to say, *Some people get powerful, then they mess things up and other people take over, until they mess up.* I used to like history but wanted out of the class in the worst way since my own history lesson, Nicole Snider, sat two chairs away.

I tried not to look, but I wasn't that strong. It would've taken all the muscle mass in Brody's arms to stop me from turning my head to look at her. Like most everyone in the school, she wore the red and white game-day colors. Under her bright red sweater, she had on a white blouse with a button-down collar tucked into black button-fly jeans. Whenever she'd worn these jeans before, I couldn't help but focus on one round gold button, almost at the crotch—no man's land thanks to the purity pledge.

Today as I sat in history class, I thought about Nicole's future with Kyle and couldn't help but wonder if that promise was a lie. The truth is like oxygen: it's all around but you can't see it. You take it on faith that it is there and you would die without it. But lies are like poison gas: you can't see *it* either, but if you pay attention, you can sometimes smell it before it's too late.

Lomax rambled on about Athens, like any of it mattered. He spoke in a monotone voice that went well with his monochrome brown outfit. I finally snapped back to attention when he asked the rare question. While my hand stayed down, half of the others' in the room went up. It was like he had said, *Okay, raise your hand if you have a future.*

When Nicole answered Lomax's question, it was overwhelming. I wasn't thinking so much about her voice speaking, as I was about her mouth against Kyle's ear, not mine; of her lips touching Kyle's lips, not mine. I could feel and smell them together, and that imagined touch and smell was like throwing another log on a fire, adding another brick in a wall, or hammering another nail in the coffin. She was the last straw.

"Mr. Lomax?" I raised my hand like a drowning victim calling for help.

"Yes, Mr. Salisbury. You have a comment about Athenian government?" Lomax said.

"I need a bathroom pass," I replied, embarrassed but unbowed. "Now."

Mr. Lomax sighed, which, other than writing on the board in something resembling hieroglyphics, was what Lomax did best. I grabbed the pass from the desk and walked outside. The minute the door closed behind me, I bent over trying to catch my breath.

I walked toward the bathroom farthest away from the classroom to give me the most possible time out of class. I kept thinking about Nicole signing the purity pledge and wondered how many other girls at school had done the same. I know I couldn't do it; I don't know many guys at school who could. It'd be like promising not to take a piss in the morning.

I wanted to confess to Nicole, tell her, *I know you think I'm sex crazed, but I can't help myself.* Everywhere I looked—at school, on TV, on the net, or in my own DVD player—were girls I wanted. Ex-Dad was no help: at his apartment, he couldn't let a TV show or even an ad go by without some dirty remark about a girl on the screen. So it was no surprise when at his apartment, I found, watched, and then stole the DVD *Filthy First Times #18.*

He never said anything to me about it. I figured either he didn't notice it was missing or was too embarrassed to confront me about it. I kept the stolen DVD hidden away, although I lived in fear Mom would find it, or catch me red-handed watching it one-handed. After each viewing, I promised myself I would throw it away, but then I'd give in and watch just one scene, then another, and another. Sometimes I'd go a few days, but rarely longer.

I'd hinted to Brody about it, but finally showed it to him the first day of summer vacation after ninth grade. It was just the two of us. Something about Garrett was bothering me, and our smackdown was just days away. And while Aaron had bought his way into the circle, I still didn't trust him totally. When Brody said his mom was out, I brought over the DVD for him to see. Even before the first scene ended, we both felt embarrassed watching it together—lying on the floor, alternating between cracks and moments of silence, shock, and awe. I guess we watched so intently that we didn't hear the door open and his mom come in. I wondered how her fire alarm-volume voice didn't wake the dead when she saw what was on her TV screen.

"What the hell is going on here?" she shouted as she dropped bags of groceries on the floor. Brody made a futile dive for the DVD player, but it was too late. "Oh my God, I don't believe this. I don't believe this!"

"Shut up!" Brody shouted. I didn't know who he was talking to, but I assumed it was me.

"What is the meaning of this?" His mom charged into the living room, unplugged the TV, and then pushed it on the floor for a glass-shattering finale. I breathed a quick silent sigh of relief that she only smashed the TV, not the DVD player, so *Filthy First Timers #18* was safe.

"Mick Salisbury, I would never have guessed. When your mother hears—"

"It's not Mick's fault," Brody said. He spoke the lie like it was the pure truth. I just looked at the floor, memorizing the pattern of the well-worn brown shag carpet. "Mick had nothing to do with it. He didn't even want to be here. It was all my idea."

"I don't believe you." Brody's mom retreated to the kitchen and reached for the phone.

"I swear on Dad's grave, it's true." I sat in awe at Brody's powers of deceit.

"You're grounded for one month," she said as she moved away from the phone, and her voice finally returned to its normal high volume. "One month, you understand?"

"Yes," Brody mumbled, and he tried to hide a smile.

"No television, no phone calls, nothing," she continued, then walked toward a broom closet in the kitchen. "And you're going back to Mass with me every Sunday. And confession."

"Right," Brody said, finally catching my eye. When Brody's mother turned around to get something out of the closet, Brody quickly ejected the DVD. He handed it back to me, and I buried it under my shirt. Brody leaned toward me and whispered, "We're cool, right?"

Brody's mom turned around, still angry. "And clean this mess up!"

Brody just grunted, while I hid my guilty eyes from Brody's innocent mother.

"And you help him," Brody's mom said sharply to me. "And then I don't want to see you over here for the rest of the summer, you understand me?"

I also just grunted. I knew his mom never followed through (and she didn't this time either. I was back over a week later). She shook her head again, then left the room. I started to speak, but Brody whispered, "Shut up." As we swept up the mess, I knew that although a lot of glass had shattered that day, our friendship was sealed forever.

I took my time returning to class. I was in no hurry to sit so close to Nicole yet be so far away from her. As I walked back through the hallways, I wished I was on the beach, walking in the sand. In the sand, you could see your footprints and always know where you've been and what you've seen. In life, you only had your memory, and it seemed to me the worse the memory, the bigger it was in your mind. I didn't think I could have worse memories than cheating on Nicole and Dad cheating on Mom. I didn't know as I walked back into history class that the evening would end with the worst memory of all, and footprints left in blood, not sand.

Why do guys think about sex all the time?

I thought once I had a girlfriend that things would be differ-ent. I didn't know that while I'd promised myself I would stop, Nicole had taken a pledge of her own. It was August 6, my birthday, when we'd slipped into the back row of the movie theater and made out, just like I'd imagined. Even though our tongues tangled, Nicole kept my hands from feeling anything other than her back or brushing the hair from her eyes. I was exploding with lust and frustration. On the screen, bodies tossed in the sheets, while in the seats, the heat rose in me like water steaming on a sun-baked street. After the movie, we went outside to wait for our ride. The sun was shining brightly, and I was blinded by the contrast to the darkness of the movie theater moments ear-lier and the even darker words coming from Nicole's mouth. At her church, she said, she'd taken a purity pledge not to have sex until marriage. She explained to me about her church, her faith, and this pledge, which meant not just sex itself, but most everything else beyond what we'd done just moments ago. I wanted to persuade her to break her pledge, but for all my imaginary conversations, I couldn't find the words, so I nodded in agreement. What I couldn't explain to her, and what I still don't understand, is the answer to my question: why do guys think about sex all the time?

Sixth Period

I'm not a big fan of poetry. If we could study real poets like Led Zeppelin's Robert Plant, then I might actually pay attention to my English teacher, Mrs. Kirby. But to her, poetry's about boring dead white guys yearning for urns and roads not taken, instead of stairways to heaven.

We once had a writer visit our class—some guy who thought he was a lot funnier than he really was—and he said one thing that really stuck with me. Most writing, he told us, was about asking two questions: How come? or What if? Robert Frost was caught up in the "what if," but then, like now, I stirred the ashes and traced the path of "how come."

Not that I didn't ask "what if" a lot. I spent a good part of my day having "what if" conversations, thinking of things I wanted to say or should have said. And then there was my favorite "what if," just looking around the room at every girl and wondering: what if? There's Terri, Nicole's best friend. She's not gorgeous, but still too pretty for me. Terri, Shelby—there's no girl in that English class I wouldn't want to be with, at least once. It's part of me that I can't explain, this big hulking physical part of me that overwhelms everything else that I can't find words for. I wondered how I managed to get through the day without saying anything to these girls. I wondered where my self-control came from, since ex-Dad had none, and I'd shown with Roxanne how easy it was to lose it. You could believe one thing and in a second, under the wrong circumstances and right temptations, act differently.

I was lost in my imaginary words when very real ones came from the front of the room. "Mr. Salisbury, please entertain us with your thoughts about the poem," Mrs. Kirby bellowed. We'd handed in our papers at the start of class, so I was trying to remember what I wrote.

"What I thought?" I mumbled, stalling for time, and kicking myself under the desk. I'd forgotten this was one way Mrs. Kirby tried to catch people who didn't read the books, stories, or poems. She would make them talk out loud, then compare what they said to what they wrote. I hoped against hope that Brody at least read what I wrote, but the look in her eyes made me think he hadn't. Her expression told me she thought I'd done something wrong. No doubt she'd glanced at the paper Brody handed in last period and figured out he didn't write it, which made me her number one suspect.

"We're waiting," Mrs. Kirby said.

"Um, it was okay, I guess," I said, to much laughter.

"Yes, continue," Mrs. Kirby replied, sounding bored.

"To be honest, I thought it was stupid," I said as hands shot up amid much laughter.

She ignored the hands and instead asked me, "And what is stupid about it?"

I paused and looked around the room until I spotted Terri. Her eyes darted away like a deer hearing a gun shot, but I knew this was an open door. "Well, the guy's saying something about making choices," I mumbled, unsure of myself at first.

"Oh, you mean he's not talking about roads," Mrs. Kirby added, sounding amused. I was distracted by hands going up all around the room, but I was the one drowning, not them.

"Right, he's talking about choices," I said, this time a little louder. I'm smart, but I know I don't have that "look," the one that would make teachers think I was a good student. I often wondered if that was really what made all the difference. Not who you are, but what you look like. If I was as good looking or preppy as Kyle, no way would Nicole have dumped me. Just thinking about Kyle was like gasoline poured on a fire. I know I cheated on Nicole, but the world cheated me first, so I said, "It's about a guy who gets cheated and feels bad."

"Cheated?" The tone in Mrs. Kirby's voice was one of disbelief. "Explain, please."

"Frost seems to be saying that in life you come to forks in the road and make decisions about what to do." I could barely get the words from my throat. "I don't think it works that way."

"What way?" Mrs. Kirby asked like she was actually interested.

"Well, you know, I think the majority of your decisions are mostly made for you," I said, my confidence growing. "It's not what choice you make, it's who you are."

"But doesn't everyone have choices?" she asked. Hands shot up again, but I wouldn't surrender.

"We don't know anything about this guy in the poem.

I don't think everybody gets to make the same choices." My mind flashed back to ex-Dad in his new SUV; the Scarecrow in his straw hat. "Before you make a choice, all this stuff happens, and Frost doesn't talk about it."

"You said 'cheated'—you still have to tell us what you mean," Mrs. Kirby said.

"That's what I'm saying." I paused but wanted to scream in frustration because I couldn't make people understand me. "You hear how everybody is equal, but that's a lie. If somebody's rich, then somebody else is poor. And if you don't have stuff . . ." I paused again. I couldn't bring myself to list the things I didn't have that the Kyle and the Whitney World have; I couldn't bring myself to tell everyone how inadequate I felt even in an unfair world.

"And?"

"And if you don't have stuff, it's like somebody cheated you out of it," I said.

"Stuff?" She tried not to laugh at my use of such an unpoetic word while discussing poetry.

"But it's more than that," I said and I wondered if people actually saw the lightbulb go on over my head like in some cartoon. "Who you are determines which choices you get to make. So, while everybody has choices, the less stuff you have, the fewer choices you get. That's what I mean by cheated."

"Very interesting," Mrs. Kirby said. I believe she smiled at me for the first time ever.

"Um, one more thing," I said. Mrs. Kirby looked amused again, no doubt wondering who had taken over my body.

"Continue, please," she said, then motioned for others to put down their raised hands.

"I think the poem's also about regret," I said, then turned away from the teacher to look right at Terri, so she could tell Nicole. "I think the poem is about when you make the wrong choices, feel bad, and wish you could just undo it. Wish you could make things right."

"Very interesting, Mick, I look forward to reading your paper," Mrs. Kirby said. I stood there for a moment before sitting down, wondering if Terri would deliver the message to Nicole. But she just looked bored and her eyes were like a vacuum pulling every single soul out of the room. Only I was left, feeling totally alone in the world. Mrs. Kirby saw me maybe for the first time as a bright and engaged student, but as I caught a glimpse of myself in Terri's soul-sucking stare, I saw something different. I wasn't Mick Salisbury, I wasn't even Pool Boy or 151. In her eyes and those of Nicole, I was a pathetic, lonely, and hopeless figure; I was a scarecrow.

Do you have a nickname?

I guess you could say that Mick is a nickname, but that's not what I mean. I'm talking about nicknames like 151 or Pool Boy, tags Brody stuck on me. I don't mind 151, although I don't really like that other people in school know about it. It's funny, in junior high, you wanted everyone to think you were cool enough and old enough to get drunk, but now, it's not something you share, it's something you do. Pool Boy I don't like because it is kind of a put-down name, but Brody's the only one who uses it, so I guess that's okay. Worst nickname I ever heard was one this kid back in seventh grade, Robert Smith, had. I didn't really know him well, most people didn't. He was one of those kids who just shows up at school every day, nothing special about him. One day in history class, we're taking a test about Indian tribes. It's really quiet in the room, and he farts really loud. Everybody heard it. Somebody asked, "Who did that?" Brody, who was sitting right next to him, points at Robert Smith and says, "It was Chief Brown Cloud." Everybody laughed, maybe even the teacher. Smith looked like he wanted to die right then, and for the rest of the school year everybody called him Chief Brown Cloud, even me. I knew it was mean, but he just seemed so hopeless that it was easy to do because he couldn't do anything about it. He transferred schools at the end of the year. Thinking about him now, what strikes me is this: in one second, his life changed forever. It wasn't something he did on purpose, just an accident. But from that moment, his life spun in a different direction. Every day you live through exactly 86,400 seconds, but a stupid mistake or accident or bad judgment in just one of those seconds can change every other second of every minute of every day for the rest of your life. And it can happen to anyone: it doesn't matter if you're the president of the United States, Chief Brown Cloud, Mick Salisbury, Brody Warren, Aaron Bishop, or the Scarecrow.

Seventh Period

Looking down from the rocking bleachers filled with Dragon pride, I couldn't care less as the cheerleaders proclaimed, "We've got spirit, yes we do, we've got spirit, how about you?" The football players ran out onto the gym floor while the band played the school song. I wished I could slip on my jPod to drown them out, but instead I waved for Brody to join me in the last row of the bleachers closest to the front door. I hated pep rallies, but I didn't mind missing my seventh period computer class where Mr. Scott insisted on teaching us things we all already knew.

"Dude, what's up?" I asked, and then tensed for Brody's hard backslap greeting.

"Nothing," Brody said. He looked glum and kept his hands at his sides.

"What's wrong?" I asked.

Brody just stared at his beat-up boots. "Kirby nailed me for cheating!"

"Shit!"

"Don't worry, man, I didn't rat you out," Brody said as he jammed his finger into my chest. "I'm gonna blow her tires or something."

"Dude, don't make it worse," I said, but I wanted to say, *Brody, it's not her fault that you decided to cheat. Take responsibility for your own actions, be a man.* But I said nothing. I knew there are two kinds of friends in the world: those who tell you what you want to hear, and those who tell you what you need to hear. Brody's all about want, never about need.

"It's not like other people don't do it too," Brody said as he flipped Mrs. Kirby the finger from a distance. Ever since I got kicked off the football team, if I do something wrong, I get in trouble."

"I know," I mumbled as I spotted Nicole and Kyle on the other side of the gym. I wondered what would happen if Kyle cheats on Nicole. I also wondered how Kyle and Nicole got together so soon after our breakup. Had she cheated on me first? Maybe he had already had his taste. Kyle, that sad bastard, doesn't know that a little taste is all he's gonna get.

"Shit, shit, shit!" Brody punched himself in the head through his long, tangled hair.

"Dude, don't worry about it," I said. "Tonight around seven, it's all forgotten."

"Right," Brody said, then raised an invisible glass. We stayed silent for a while, letting the noise of the pep rally surround us. When Coach Simpson spoke, Brody looked agitated.

"You miss it?" I said, as I stared up at last year's division banner hanging from the gym ceiling.

"What? Football?" Brody responded.

"Yeah, playing football." Brody never talked about it much after he got kicked off the team other than swearing revenge on whoever ratted him out for breaking the Words of Honor oath.

"I miss playing," Brody said. "I miss making those tackles, smacking pads, yeah, I miss playing the game, but I don't miss being on the team. Don't miss rules. Don't miss practices."

"Bet you miss the cheerleaders," I said as I pointed to Lita Gomez. The only Latino girl on the squad, she's the odd one out, so I suspected she would be Brody's favorite.

"Maybe," Brody said, then laughed. "I miss getting As, not getting in trouble. No way Kirby would have called me out if I was still on the team. People kick you when you're down."

"True," I said as I felt all of Brody's resentment wash over me. I didn't hate the jocks, like the stoners or the artsy kids in theater did. I don't like sports much, but ex-Dad was always taking me to games or making me watch them with him on TV, and I accepted it as my manly duty.

"Well, we'll have our own celebration tonight, right, 151?" Brody said with a hard backslap.

"Dude, I'm so ready. I bet Aaron's ready to go again, too." My eyes scanned the crowd for the third member of the Rum Drinker's Local 151, but Aaron was nowhere to be found.

"Something was seriously wrong with ATM last night," Brody said, then rose.

"The dad thing," I muttered, kind of half-hoping Brody didn't hear me.

"Come on, let's sneak out of here," Brody said as he gestured for me to join him. We started down the bleachers through the sea of red Dragon jackets worn by football fans who'd once cheered for Brody and now turned their back on him, which is something I knew I'd never do.

Just as we hit the last step, the cheerleaders got the

crowd fired up again. Brody looked like he wanted to spit, but instead he said, "It's just a stupid football game. It's not like it's life or death."

I grunted and thought then how most decisions were never that simple: life or death.

What do you think death feels like?

I read once that the difference in weight between a living body and a dead body is 21 grams. It's not like I know what that means, but it doesn't sound like a lot. What is in those 21 grams: your soul? Where does it go? Is it like a puff of smoke? Do you go toward a light? We'll never know because the dead don't talk to us, they just haunt us. Our ghost-to-be lies in front of us, arms outstretched, legs almost curled underneath him, and his tongue dangling from his almost toothless mouth. Even if he was alive, I doubt he could have breathed, because it felt like we were sucking up all of the oxygen in the cluttered, filthy space. What was his last breath like? What is the moment of realization when you understand that you're about to die? Is it a thing of stark beauty or indescribable fear? Does it matter how you die? Is it better to go slowly with cancer eating away at your body, or to go quickly: in an auto accident crushing your bones and organs like a trash compacter, or a violent death at the hands of another, wielding a gun, knife, fist, boot, or brick? Is it better to know when and how you're going to die, or to have it come upon you suddenly and unexpectedly? As I sit with my arms wrapped around my knees, and my head hanging low ready to vomit again, I want to rock myself back toward birth. If I'd never been born, then I wouldn't have to die. If I'd never been born, then I wouldn't have ever killed.

I made my way to my locker after the prep-pep rally, walking mostly uphill against the teeming Red Dragon masses crowding the hallway. Brody was at the office getting his punishment, while I was caught in a cloud of negative thoughts. Maybe it's how that day started with Mom's questions about homecoming and some unstated expectation that I was failing to reach. Maybe it was seeing Whitney so beautiful at the bus stop or Rex so ugly to me before gym class. Maybe it was the stupid loudness of the rally or the silent loneliness I felt whenever I saw Nicole. Maybe it was all of these things, maybe it was nothing, but I'd never felt so pissed off. After tossing my books into the bottom of my locker, I loudly slammed the door on the day. The sound catapulted me into thoughts of tonight—drinking with Brody and Aaron, where nobody had expectations of me and there was nobody to answer to or judge me.

"You lock it?" I heard Aaron shout to get my attention. It was odd to hear Aaron's voice at that volume. While Brody almost always yelled, I'd never known Aaron to, unless he was drunk.

"Sorry," I said, then turned around to reenter the locker combination.

"No problem," Aaron replied. I was amazed that Aaron, who had been so angry, so loud, and so drunk the night before could be so calm, so soft-spoken, and so far from hungover.

"What time? The bus leaves at seven," I said, using fin-ger quotes around the word *bus*.

"Wanna meet up around six forty-five?" Aaron replied. "I gotta spend stepdad time before."

My eyes bounced back a strange mix of envy and sym-pathy. "You going home now?"

"No, gonna go study," Aaron said as he loaded up his backpack. That's what hard classes and high expectations get you: strong arms and a surefire way to disappointment.

"Gotta run," I said, then sprinted off toward the bus. I joyously pulled down crepe paper and stomped on balloons as I left the building, trampling on a little of that Dragon false pride.

Outside, I hung back by the flagpole as other riders gathered for the bus. Rusty and Bob were absent, probably in some pregame team meeting. While I felt bad about Brody getting kicked off that team and all, I liked having him around to hang with at school and after.

"You catching this ride?" I pointed to the bus as Brody slouched toward me.

"Nah, I'm hitting the weight room," Brody said, then slapped the muscle on his left arm with his right hand. "Be my last chance to move some iron after school for a while."

"How bad?" I asked, but didn't want to look Brody in the eye about this topic.

"I got a week's detention, plus I've got to rewrite the pa-per," Brody said.

"Sorry, man, you know it's my fault. If I would have told you I wouldn't write it for you, then none of this—" I started, but Brody was having none of it.

"Damn Kirby's fault, not yours or mine. She needs to get a life. So I cheated. If she wants to catch cheaters, she should spend time there." Brody pointed at the football field.

"I guess," I said. I knew I wasn't to blame, but I was drowning in guilt anyway.

"See you tonight," Brody said, then started to walk away.

"Six forty-five, right?" I reminded Brody, knowing I'd end up waiting for him regardless.

"No, Mick, 151!" Brody's laugh was almost as loud as the crowd boarding the bus.

I waited until the Whitney World got on before I entered the bus. I kept my eyes on the floor, looking past gum wrappers and lost pencils, toward the seat behind Whitney. I slipped in easily, like I belonged. Whitney never blinked; she was busy talking with Shelby. I put my headphones on, so it looked like I was listening to music rather than listening in on them.

When I heard Whitney mention math, I treated it like Brody used to treat a fumble.

"When's the next test in math?" I asked her.

"Next week, I think." She sounded unsure of herself, or maybe she was unsure of me.

"Do you study a lot for that class?" I said, then leaned forward. I was making a big show of removing the headphones.

"I guess." Whitney's tone sounded more annoyed than embarrassed. I wanted to say, *Look, I just don't know how to talk to girls, but I'm really a nice guy.* But then I imagined her response: *From what I heard, you know very little about girls, and have little to do it with.*

"It helps if you look at the board in class sometimes," Shelby said, then giggled. And I knew I was busted. I didn't say anything but my blushing face acted as my confession.

"Maybe," I mumbled, then stood up and rambled toward the back of the bus feeling like everyone was staring at me: my humiliation seemed total as Shelby whispered something to Whitney, who laughed and then turned to the girl next to her. It was a tidal wave of embarrassment washing over me. The bus lurched forward as I walked against inertia to seek out Dave Wilson. Wilson was back in the same place I'd left him this morning, face against the glass. I kicked his seat gently.

"What?" Dave said, eyes still closed, obviously aware of my presence, no doubt because of the smell. I wondered if it was the stink from not showering after gym or from the shit that Shelby dumped on me. My odor was mysterious; Dave Wilson's was obvious stoner.

"You got a smoke?" I asked, trying to retain some sense of cool self.

"Sure, dude," Dave said as he opened his eyes.

"I owe you."

"I'll put it in my book," Dave said, then laughed. A stoner laugh. Wilson reached into his long trench coat and pulled out a pack of unfiltered Camels. He handed me a single stick.

"Thanks." I put the smoke behind my ear, then moved back up near the front of the bus. I didn't even stop to look at Whitney—shouldn't I be looking at the board?—and waited for the next stop, which happened to be at WindGate. I breathed a smoke-free sigh of relief that Roxanne wasn't on the bus as I exited with a few others. I watched the trailer parkers head toward their tiny homes, then watched the bus with the Whitney World pull away toward my neighborhood's nice houses. Standing alone by the side of the road, I waited until the bus was out of sight before I pulled out my white lighter, a gift from Brody for my birthday. I knew Brody loved the lighter, so it really was about the thought, not the thing itself. Ex-Dad gave me a bunch of stuff, including tickets to a Lion's football game next weekend, but Brody's beat-up lighter meant the most.

I cupped my hand against the wind, then lit the smoke. I wasn't scared of being caught by anyone. What was Mom going to say? Smoking is wrong. I knew ex-Dad was at work. He was always at work or pretending to be when he lived with us. I pulled the smoke deep into my lungs and started the long, lonely mile-plus walk toward my deserted house.

Then I saw him by the side of the road: the Scarecrow.

He had his HUNGRY VET, PLEASE HELP, GOD BLESS sign out, but few cars stopped. No doubt the ones that did were like ex-Dad, hurling insults rather than pitching pennies.

The cigarette dangled from my lips as I reached into my pockets looking for change. My wallet was free of pictures, love notes from Nicole, phone numbers, or even unused condoms. Those were stored with the *First Times* DVD deep in my closet. I found a couple of quarters, then walked toward the Scarecrow.

With each step, my make-believe dialogue built. I wanted

to say, *Man, how did you get like this? What happened to you?* I had no idea what to do with my life, but I was figuring out pretty fast what I didn't want to be. I didn't want to be some nine-to-five GM jerk like ex-Dad; I didn't want to work at some clothing store like Mom where the world orbited around appearance. I didn't know what kind of job I wanted, and sometimes I wondered if I'd even get a job. Last year in social studies class with Mr. Daunt, rather than reading about the dead civilizations of Greece and Rome, we read about current events. Mr. Daunt would bring in the *Flint Journal* and open my eyes to what was around me. Flint was becoming a modern city of ruins.

I threw my coins in the Scarecrow's mostly empty can. The echo of a metallic clank rang in my ears, while my eyes focused on him. He looked back at me, and I felt the urge to flee.

With each slap of my shoes against the pavement, the anger within me raced. I ran past Whitney's house, where she was no doubt still laughing at Shelby's smackdown of me. I ran past Brody's house; no doubt he was still at school pumping iron and building up a thirst. I ran down our vacant driveway and didn't stop running until I was inside. I was out of breath, and drowning in rage. I slammed the door behind me loud enough to rattle the windows.

As I charged through the kitchen, I saw money on the table, a message on the machine, and felt the crushing feelings of disappointment, embarrassment, and humiliation closing in from all four walls. Everyone needed a place to be, but I was still shopping for a place to put my anger. It was backing up inside me, deeper and darker. I'd put my hand into the Bunsen burner this morning, but that only provided a temporary release for this fiery fury running through my veins. I took off the bandage and looked at my burned skin; the pain felt right as I reached for the phone to dial Nicole. I needed her acceptance to save me from my terrible day, or her humiliating rejection to push me over the edge.

What's the most humiliated you've ever felt?

It was the first and last summer I played little league base-ball. I was eight, and it was a strangely cold day with a light drizzle on a late June afternoon. I was waiting to hit, or rather to take three swings then sit down, when I noticed my parents in the stands. I felt stupid—both of them taking the time to watch me fail at sports. Dad looked bored; I could almost hear sighs from where I stood in the on-deck circle. Mom looked worried, like something other than rain-filled dark clouds was bothering her. I tried to focus on tak-ing my swings, which didn't seem to kill the butterflies in my stomach, it just sent them fluttering throughout my body. When the guy in front of me hit a double, I felt even more pressure. It was the last inning, the score was tied, and there were two outs; a hit would win the game. If there was anyone left to pinch-hit, I'm sure the coach would have put him in, but I was the last one in the game. I was almost crying I was so nervous, and I didn't see Mom come onto the field until she was in the on-deck circle with me. In front of all the guys on the team and the other team, she handed me this bright yellow windbreaker to put on, to protect me from the cold. I tried to tell her to go away, but she was hav-ing none of it. Later, I told her how embarrassing it had been, to do that in front of my friends, but she'd told me something then that she's repeated more than once so I'd al-ways remember it: Mick, your friends will come and go, but you've only got one mother, who will protect you no matter what.

4:00 p.m.

As the phone rang, I stared at my raw, damaged skin. When Nicole's machine picked up—You've reached the Sniders. Please leave us a message and we'll get back with you. Have a blessed day—I panicked. I didn't know what I wanted to say, so I left a message of ten seconds of heavy silence. I was lucky that Nicole didn't answer, I knew I wasn't ready. Examining my hand, I felt fortunate. Lucky the burn wasn't worse, but luckier that Mr. Gates sent me to the school nurse instead of to the school counselor. The counselors live to pick at scabs and open wounds.

I remembered right after my parent's broke up, Mom took me to a counselor to help me, in her words, "begin healing." I did my mute act, the one Mom knew all too well, and never said anything. What I should have said was, *Doctor, I know my parents are splitting up. I know it's not my fault, but I know they'll both always blame me anyway. I know it's Dad's fault, but he won't ever say those words, and Mom won't ever really be okay until he does. So, I betrayed my father; served him right for cheating on Mom and betraying her. You see, the truth didn't set me free at all. Maybe once everything is even, once my mom betrays me, then we'll all be healed.*

I put down the phone and went into the dining room to retrieve my allowance on the table. In addition to two ten-dollar bills—my pay for doing chores that I would have done for free just to help Mom out around the house—there was a white envelope with my name on it. Unlike ex-Dad, Mom didn't make me count the change or account for every penny misspent. I laughed when I saw my name on the envelope: who else did she think the envelope could be for? I laughed harder, trying to guess what Mom was thinking most of the time. I ripped the envelope open and saw three crisp twenty-dollar bills and a note that read,

Mick, I'm sorry about this morning. I called the school and they told me how much homecoming tickets cost. We'll go shopping tomorrow for a handsome new suit for you to wear that will make us both proud. Love you, Mom.

I grabbed some cold pizza leftovers and a Coke from the fridge, then sat at the table, feeling lonely and sorry for myself, thinking about Mom. I wished I could tell her, *Mom, thanks for the cash, but I don't think I'm going to homecoming. You see, Nicole and I broke up. Wait, that's not true, let me tell you the whole truth for once: She dumped me. I cheated on her, just like Dad cheated on you. I still don't know why I did it. I so don't want to be like Dad.*

I slurped down the Coke and finished off the pizza. I took a deep breath, then dialed Nicole's number again. As the phone rang, the words formed. *Nicole, I know you don't want to talk to me and I don't blame you. Just give me a second chance. Just let me—*but the machine picked up again and cut off my thoughts. This time I left a simple message, "Hey, Nicole, it's Mick. Can you call me? It's kinda important," and hung up, doubting every word. Should I have said my last name? Does she even remember my number?

A few minutes passed, then I dialed the number again. This one counted. *Listen, it's my turn to pledge to you. I'll never betray you again.* But the machine picked up again. My message, "It's Mick, gimme a call," was shorter while my rage grew deeper. I dialed every five minutes and alternated between leaving short messages and hanging up, between feeling angry and sad; between love and hate. It might be a thin line between those two, so I had to steer myself back on the right path.

I was just about to give up, when the phone rang, shaking me like thunder. I caught my breath on the first ring, thought of what to say on the second and third—*Nicole, we need to talk, I have so much to say to you*—took a final deep breath on the fourth, and picked up on the fifth.

"Hey," I answered the best I could with my heart and head weighing down my tongue.

"Is this Mick Salisbury?" a booming male voice asked.

I grunted acknowledgment.

"This is Joseph Snider, Nicole's father." The edge of the hurricane shouted through the phone. "Stop bothering my daughter. If you call again, I'll call the police. Do you understand?"

Can you actually hear or feel your heart break?

For me, the answer was yes. Although the worst feeling wasn't in my heart, but in my guts. It felt like they were on fire. It was the first day of school, the day after the party at Rex's house, the day my life as I knew it and wanted it to be ended. I knew that Nicole was getting back into town late, so I wouldn't have a chance to talk to her before the first day of school. That may have been one of the longest nights of my life, my head swimming in rum, trying to drown out what I'd done with Roxanne. I kept telling myself that it didn't really happen, that it was a dream or maybe a nightmare. I told myself that nobody saw it or, if they did, nobody would tell Nicole. I told myself to relax, but I couldn't. The heavy burden of the lie was like a weight across my chest, crushing my ribs, which cut into my heart. In the morning, everything was fine. We saw each other before school, made plans to sit together at lunch, and talked about having history class together after lunch. But I was history by then. Nicole was waiting for me by my locker at lunch; she must have gotten out of class early. I could tell she'd been crying, but I refused to believe it until she said, "Mick, I hate you." Before I could lie, she told me what I had done with Roxanne at the party. Before I could explain or ask who told on me, she said she didn't want to see me ever again. Before I could breathe, she told me that I was a terrible person and she wished I was dead. Before I could agree, she was gone. Gone from my sight, gone from my life. We'd see each other in history class, but we had no future. As I stood by my locker, the sound of her footsteps echoing in the hallway, filling my ears, no tears filled my eyes even though I felt like crying. Instead, I let the anger flood in: anger at myself, anger at Roxanne, but most of all, anger at the person who told Nicole about Roxanne. What right did they have to ruin my life? What kind of person would do something like that? I didn't have a mirror in the locker and I didn't need one to know what kind of person would do that: a person like me.

5:00 p.m.

I wanted to hurl the phone through the kitchen window and shatter the glass. I wanted to then roll in the sharp shards, opening a thousand tiny cuts to help the blood leave my body.

I was frozen in my hot rage, nowhere to run, nowhere to hide. Even slamming the door over and over in time to the cranked up *Dark Side of the Moon* CD offered no release. I called Brody's house, but he was still at school. I left a message to meet up at Space Invaders in an hour. I tried to sleep, but sleep and salvation from pain took different roads. I resolved never to ask out another girl, never to fall in love, never to take the risk. I cracked all my fingers and toes, the snap, crackle, and pop of the joints—liquid exploding, Mr. Gates said—sounded like fire.

I looked at the clock; the square red numbers taunted me. I decided on one more futile act of frustration. I dialed the phone again, but this time there's no machine, only the helpful voice that answered loudly because the background noise was enough to wake the dead and dying: "Thank you for calling Chico's, the premier women's clothing experience featuring exceptional service and one-of-a-kind styles. How can we help you?"

"I need to speak to Linda Salisbury," I mumbled.

"One moment, please." The chipper voice clipped off the words, annoyance replacing exuberance. I braced myself to hear the hold message of sale items and bad music. I thought that was what I needed: to put my life on hold. To not have to go to school or be in love or even hang with friends, just to be in some sort of suspended state until I figured things out.

"She's with customers right now, could she—"

"I'll hold."

There was no acknowledgment, just the return of comforting sounds. I thought about Mom waiting on people who made five times as much as she does even if she worked five times harder.

"Mick, what's wrong?" Mom sounded out of breath.

I wanted to say, *Mom, everything is wrong right now, can you tell me what to do?* But no words came; I couldn't tell her I just called to hear her voice, to calm me down, to set me right.

"Mick, I'm really busy, what is it?"

"Um, I just wanted to tell you something," I said, trying to talk fast. "It's an away football game, so I might be home late, that's all."

There was dead silence.

"Mom, thanks for the cash," I said as I stopped myself from telling the truth because it was the right thing to do. Let Mom believe I'm going to homecoming. Let her believe I was in love. Let her believe; let the lie live.

"I just want you to be happy," she said. I hoped she was smiling now. But within me, only dark clouds hovered. I wanted to shout into the phone, *Mom, you know what's the worst of all of this? I feel bad for treating you like this and lying to you. I just want you to love me and be proud of me.*

But Mom, I know that you'll always love me no matter what I do, so I guess I can do anything because I know you'll forgive me. You'll never leave or reject me, always protect me. You're powerless.

"I have to go," she said, then added a quick "I love you" but I didn't get time to respond—not with those words; they embarrassed me—or even to say, "Thanks, Mom," before she hung up.

I was getting ready to leave about ten minutes later, when the phone rang again. It was ex-Dad. He never called just to talk, so I knew it wasn't good news, just more of his bullshit.

"Hello, son," ex-Dad said, like saying the word *son* made the word mean something.

"Hey." I wouldn't return the father-son serve.

"Listen, Mick, something's come up," ex-Dad started. "So, I don't think we'll be able to get together this weekend, but we have the Lion's game next Sunday."

I just grunted, not caring about missing the court-mandated father-son bonding ritual at all.

"Like I said, it's a work thing." I recognized the untruthful tone in ex-Dad's voice.

"Homecoming's next weekend. I need money for a ticket," I said without a pause, as I thought, *You can lie to Mom all you want, but you won't do it to me, you bastard.*

"You're going?" Since I rarely responded to his constant commentary about women's bodies, I assumed ex-Dad might have wondered if I was gay. So this lie also made everyone happy.

"I need sixty dollars for tickets. Can you mail it?" I knew since my parents never talked, only exchanged e-mails and angry driveway stares, that I wouldn't get caught.

Before the words came, ex-Dad sighed, a sound I've heard most of my life. The sigh reminded me of sign language: The sigh was a shortcut symbol of ex-Dad's frustrated impatience with anything and everything that I said or did. The sigh was the smoke from the angry fire that flared up with each step I took that he disliked. "Did you ask your mother?" he finally responded.

I waited for a second; what's one lie to ex-Dad, when lies were mostly all he knew. "She doesn't have enough money," I said as I twisted the bitter truth and the guilt knife a little deeper. "Was your check late again?"

Another sigh; more smoke. "Okay, fine."

"Promise?"

One last sigh. "I promise," ex-Dad said, and I buried my laughter. I wanted to say, *Dad, is this a promise like the one you made to Mom? Like the promise you make every year about how we're going to go hunting, fishing—anything? The truth is that all your promises are lies.*

"So I'll see you," I said, then twisted it in deeper. "Unless there's another work thing." I hung up the phone, slammed every door behind me, then walked out in the fall air, the gale breeze of deceit at my back. Why should I tell the truth to someone who had lied to me all my life?

What's the hardest thing you've ever had to tell some-one?

Brody never said a word to me after Dad and the mystery woman walked away from us that day at the mall. He kind of shrugged his shoulders, saying without words, *Dude, I don't know what you should do.* We went on to the arcade, like nothing had happened. Played pool, pin-ball, racing games, the usual—even if everything in my life, in just a matter of seconds, wasn't how it used to be. On the way home, I didn't say anything. I was as mute as Brody's mom who didn't say a word while his older brothers teased Brody, pulled his hair, and called him names. Brody took it like a man, so I guess I needed to be a man, too.

Mom was sitting at the kitchen table wearing a sweater in the summer since the air conditioner was blasting. She was drinking a coffee she must have picked up from Star-bucks and making out a shopping list. I didn't get any more than two feet into the room before she knew some-thing was wrong. I told myself if she didn't ask me, I wouldn't say anything. I wouldn't lie for my father, but I wouldn't feel a need to tell the truth. But she spoke. "Mick, what's wrong?"

I tried to leave the room, but she wasn't having any of it. I tried not to talk with her, but she kept smothering me with questions. I tried, but I failed. "Mom, I have to tell you some-thing," I started, not knowing how I would finish, only knowing it would end badly.

"You can tell me anything," she said. And I did. I could almost see her brain working, putting together all my father's late nights at the office with other clues that she couldn't see because she hadn't been looking. We were both crying within a few minutes.

"I'm sorry," I said, but she wouldn't have it. She hugged me instead.

"Mick, you don't need to apologize," she said through her tears. "You did the right thing. You saw something wrong, and you told me about it."

"But Dad asked me not to," I reminded her.

"He betrayed me, Mick. You don't owe him anything," she said, tears of shock turning to sadness turning to bitterness in a matter of moments.

"But—" I started, but had nothing else to say. I felt overwhelmed by emotion. I was a victim of both circumstance and coincidence, like an accident victim finding himself in the wrong place at the wrong time. Only difference was I saw the car coming toward me, and I stepped in front of it. We talked more until our voices were raw and our eyes were dry.

As I walked into my room, my mom hugged me one more time. "Mick, you did the right thing. You told the truth. Always tell the truth, Mick, no matter what the consequences," she said, and then kissed me on the forehead for the first time in years.

I couldn't sleep that night, not just because my brain was racing, but also because of the shouts, door slams, and finally car tires squealing. I had told the truth; I had *betrayed my father, who had betrayed my mother. I can't sleep now, not just because of the stress, but because of the wondering, worrying, and waiting for the last line of the triangle to be drawn.*

Space Invaders was packed with people like Brody and me with nothing better to do. I barely caught the last bus to the mall. Before I left, I called Aaron to arrange for his stepdad to pick us up and take us to the school parking lot. From there, we'd pretend to get on a bus, before heading over to Aaron's sister's trailer.

The sound of old Rolling Stones music crashed through the speakers. "Gimme Shelter" boomed loud. I jingled the change in my pocket I'd drop in the jukebox to kick out Zeppelin. Among the mostly older out-of-high-school-not-in-college crowd, I saw Creek kids who, like Brody, Aaron, and me, lacked school spirit or maybe planned to drink spirits instead.

Brody joined me at the pool table for the ritual slaughter on green felt. Hand-eye coordination was another area where I was cheated. I also couldn't really concentrate with my brain working overtime on the events of the day. I was trying not to let this anger overwhelm me, but it was hard. So I made an attempt at humor, preparing to do one of my trademark mock interviews. Before Brody broke for the last game, I held my pool cue up close to my mouth, like it was a microphone. I found the security camera, then waved for Brody to stand by me. I showed him the camera, then started, "We're standing with Brody Warren, the teen pool wizard. Tell me, how do you do it?"

"Well, Mick, I know how to handle my stick," Brody said, then winked.

"That's what all the ladies say about you as well," I replied, then we high-fived.

"And my stick is bigger than anybody's," Brody cracked, taking hold of the fake mic.

"So you're saying pool is all about your stick, and the balls?" I was trying not to laugh.

"You gotta control your balls," Brody said, then grabbed his crotch.

"As a matter of fact, don't you—" I started, but Brody cut me off.

"Dude, this interview is so over, look at that!" Brody said as he jabbed his elbow into my ribs then pointed to a hot blond girl standing next to the jukebox. She was wearing an old leather jacket and a brand new kiss-me, bloodred lipstick smile. "I bet she's a filthy first timer."

I was uncomfortable with Brody's macho male bonding, even if I was more than used to it. "Why don't you to talk to her, Brody?" I told him.

"She's all yours!" Brody shouted over the music, through the dozens of conversations, and all the way to the ceiling. He bumped me out of the way, took the shot, sunk three on the break, and let out a loud yell. All eyes turned to our table, and I locked eyes with the blond.

"No way," I said, but Brody pushed the pool cue into the back of my right leg.

"I dare you," Brody said. He accented the pronoun with his second shot, a bank job that knocked in another two balls, more than Brody implied I owned. "You've lost *this* game already."

I flipped off Brody, who just laughed, then I started down the long, lonely road from our table to the jukebox. I heard Brody cracking balls and cracking up in the background. I told myself it's a dare and it's truth: truth is I'm gonna have to get up my nerve to ask out Whitney since Nicole was gone forever. I needed some practice, and this girl was available. Right place and time.

"Hey, anything good?" I asked, trying to be cool even as I felt the sweat on my brow. The heat of the crowded pool hall and my nerves had my sweat glands working overtime.

"Depends," the girl replied. She unzipped the leather jacket, then put her hands on her hips. She was wearing two tank tops—a black one under a white one—a pair of big green cargo pants, red Converse All-Stars, and that kiss-me smile. I tried to look at her face, but my eyes would not focus. Breasts of any size, and hers were perfect, were magnets to my steely green eyes.

"My boy dared me to talk with you," I whispered, then pointed back toward Brody.

"And what did he tell you to say?" Her tone was sassy, not scared. She flicked her head back to get the hair out of her eyes.

"We didn't get that far; I didn't think I'd get this far," I said. I knew this was not as hard as talking to Whitney because I didn't know this girl: some things are easier with a stranger.

"Why is that?"

"Because when I saw you I was speechless," I said, then laughed.

"Please." She said *please* like the word was spelled with seven z's, but she was at least smiling. I was so caught up in her wide grin and perfect breasts that I didn't notice the varsity-jacket-clad Flushing High School Raider breathing down my neck.

"Got a problem?" The guy was an inch shorter than me, but looked a few years older. I knew he could kick my ass, but wondered if he knew that. Besides, the bandage on my hand made me look tough, the tiredness in my voice made me sound rough, and the anger in my soul seethed out my pores. This poor bastard didn't know I'd had a day full of last straws, and the look he gave me was the final one.

"No problem, but you interrupted me, Tad," I said dismissively, looking at the name on the jacket. The letter was from baseball, not wrestling, hockey, or football, so I felt safer.

"Leave her alone, okay?" Tad said, and I smiled at his instant retreat.

"Who is 'her'?" I asked.

"Natalie," the girl said, but Tad pushed her out of the way like he was moving a chair.

"Shut up!" Tad shouted. The girl smiled, and I winked at her. The wink was too much and Tad pushed me. Not too hard, not too soft, enough to make a point, not enough to hurt.

"Back off, mother!" Brody yelled. I turned around to see

Brody just a few feet away in almost a replay of the Rex incident at school, except Brody had his pool cue in his hands.

Two more of Natalie's noble defenders emerged. "Fuck off, long hair," one shouted.

"What did you say?" Brody shouted back.

"Brody, he said 'fuck off,'" I said, figuring the flame needed a little more fuel.

Brody swung the pool cue fast and hard against Tad's collarbone. The bone sounded like it snapped along with the cue. The others stepped back, while Natalie knelt by her fallen nonhero.

"Don't tell me what to do, motherfucker! Nobody tells me what to do!" Brody shouted. He twirled the pool cue in his right hand, dancing up and down on the balls of his feet.

"Brody, come on, he ain't worth your sweat," I said as I grabbed Brody's right arm, blocking another shot into the corner pocket of Tad's anatomy. Brody gave me a hard stare, then threw the cue down on the floor when I shouted, "Let's get out of here!"

As we ran from the arcade, I yelled over my shoulder at Natalie, "Some first impression."

We almost ran into Aaron in our mad dash from the mall. "Where's your car?" Brody yelled. My heart was pumping double time: fear on one side and released frustration on the other.

"Over there," Aaron said and pointed at his stepdad's white Ford Explorer by the curb.

"We gotta go. Now!" Brody raced off with Aaron and me in pursuit. When we got to the car, I felt all scrambled inside.

CHEATED

Brody had this huge smile on his face, while I had a question mark dangling over my head. As we drove from the mall, I couldn't help but wonder if Brody was my best friend or my worst mistake.

Do you want to know a secret?

The only thing harder than keeping a secret about yourself is keeping one for someone else. It was a Sunday afternoon last summer. Brody had spent the morning in church—his mom was insistent, especially after the porno incident a few weeks earlier—but we got together in the afternoon to shoot pool at Space Invaders. We were playing, talking, laughing, like any other time, when Brody mentioned how his dad always promised he'd buy a pool table, but never did.

"He did a lot of that," Brody said as he waited for me to break.

"A lot of what?" I asked after my break shot barely managed to shake up the table.

"Promised stuff, then never delivered," he said, then sank two on his shot. "Solids."

"I know all about that," I added. Ex-Dad was a promise-making-and-breaking machine.

"It was typical of him," Brody said as another ball fell in. "Son of a bitch lied probably from the day he was born until the day he died."

I chalked up the cue. I always felt awkward when Brody talked about his father's death. I remembered reading the article in the newspaper about the car crash, and my mother showing me the obituary in the Flint Journal. *I remembered the funeral and how different it was than ones I'd seen on TV or in movies. On TV, everybody cried. At Brody's dad's funeral, not a tear.*

"Until the day he died," Brody repeated as he tucked

the three ball into a corner pocket. "You know how he died?"

"Auto accident, right?"

"Kind of," Brody said, although he never looked at me. Instead, he lined up his shot, then smacked the cue ball into a group of solids that split like radioactive atoms.

"What do you mean?"

Brody sank two more, leaving only the eight ball and my untouched seven stripes. "Dude, I know I can trust you, right?"

We'd had such a history. I was insulted and honored by the question. I leaned forward.

"It was no accident," Brody said as he pointed toward the corner pocket.

"What do you mean?"

"We're Catholic, and suicide is a sin, so—" The smack of the white ball against the black one drowned out Brody's fading words.

"What are you saying?"

"My dad killed himself."

"How do you know?" I asked.

"I found the note." Brody had the cue ball in his hand. He was tossing it like an apple.

"What did you do?"

"What do you think I did?" Brody hurled the white ball down the length of the table. It careened off one side, then another, and another until it landed in the pocket nearest Brody.

"I burned it."

"You didn't tell anybody?"

Brody shrugged, then spoke. "My mom gets to go to bed every night thinking it was an accident. You tell me, what good would have come from telling her the truth?"

We played a few more games. Brody acted like he had confessed nothing; I was the one sinking in guilt. Guilt for not protecting my mom from an ugly truth like Brody had, and guilt for not being a better son. I felt both so honored and so weighed down by Brody's trust that I would never betray him. Like solids and stripes on the pool table, trust and guilt belonged together.

7:00 p.m.

As I stared out the smudged window of the SUV as it pulled into the crowded school parking lot jammed with Dragon football fans, all I could think about was how stupid it all was: not just football games and cheerleaders, but high school. When I was with Brody, even getting into trouble like at the arcade, I didn't feel like some stupid kid. I felt the rush of becoming a man.

"Thanks for the ride," I told Aaron's stepdad. He's this nice, balding, middle-aged man with no personality. Jumping out of the car, Brody disappeared into a group milling around the buses, so I was left with Aaron. The adrenaline still pumped through my body and poured out through my mouth. I asked Aaron something I'd wanted to for a long time. "So, what's he like?"

"Who?" Aaron answered.

"Your stepdad," I said. Conversation with Aaron and me was always awkward, especially if I asked him questions. He'd rather listen to Brody than reveal himself to us.

"He's all right, I guess," Aaron said, and then pulled up his hoodie against the wind.

"Really?" I asked. I sometimes wondered if my life would be different—and I wasn't sure for better or worse—if ex-Dad was dead like Aaron's and Brody's fathers. Maybe I would love him more, or not at all, if he wasn't around. I envied Aaron and Brody in some weird way.

"No, not really," Aaron mumbled, his eyes firmly focused on the pavement. "He must think I'm stupid or something not to know what this is all about."

"What?" I asked, but I knew. Now that his sister's out of the house, he was virtually an only child. I have this strange anger at Aaron's stepdad for moving Aaron out of the neighborhood. Where he lived—the new Lake Breeze subdivision—was full of new homes and fancy cars. It seemed like another world, even if it shared a common wooded area with WindGate. Swartz Creek's messed up that way: it is full of old trailer parks, new subdivisions, and a glaring imbalance. It's not a creek, but a river of truth about unfairness.

"This: you know, the rides, the vacations, all of it," Aaron said. "He doesn't want in to my life. He just wants in to my mom's pants."

"Dude, that's harsh."

"Dude, that's what the truth is," Aaron replied, head straight down. "Where's Brody?"

"Who knows?" I said, then surveyed the crowd for Brody's familiar head. Before I could say anything else, my world turned to white noise when I saw Whitney along with Shelby walking toward the bus.

Aaron saw the same vision. "Here's your chance."

I took a deep breath, and then started off on my second long walk of the night, telling myself I feared nothing. "Whitney, wait up!" I yelled, earning a nasty glare from Shelby. Her eyes were like barbed wire trying to keep me out of the Whitney World.

Whitney turned to face me, then spoke. "You going to the game tonight?"

"Maybe," I muttered, then pointed at the bus. "Seems I only get to see you on a bus."

"I guess," Whitney said as Shelby cleared her throat. "Hey, we have to go."

"Can I ask you something?" My head was down, palms open, heart yearning.

"We have to go," Shelby answered. "Maybe your ears don't work as well as your eyes."

"Whitney, I need a second," I said. Shelby looked at Whitney, who stared back at me.

"Save me a seat," Whitney said, then took a step back. Shelby rolled her eyes, but walked toward the bus. I was ready to say, *Whitney, I know you don't know me that well, but I really like you. Or would like to get to know you. Would you like to go to homecoming with me?*

"I have to go, can't this wait?" she said.

"Um, well, homecoming is coming up and—" I started but then saw the look on her face: a strange mix of sympathy, pity, and embarrassment. I wouldn't need to remember her rejection of my offer because I never got to make it. Her nonanswer saved my life.

"Mick, I have to go," she said as she turned and walked away. Her long blond hair was the yellow brick road not taken. Whitney was the last one on the bus, which pulled away moments later. I was left alone in the middle of a large gray parking lot with my thoughts and the imagined sound of laughter from Shelby falling over me like a cold rain. I turned on my heel then walked back to my friends. I knew by the time we saw the bottom of the bottle, I wouldn't be thinking about Whitney, Nicole, Shelby, or anyone. By the last swallow, I wanted only one thing: not to be thinking or feeling anything.

· · ·

"She blew me off, like I was garbage," I told Brody and Aaron as we left the school parking lot a few moments later.

But as the words left my mouth, I wished I could have taken them back. Brody pounded his right fist into his open left palm. "Whitney's a stuck-up bitch!" he yelled.

"Forget it. It's over," I mumbled, barely audible over the rustle of the leaves on the back road.

"You're too easy on people who treat like you shit!" Brody shouted. We wanted to stay out of sight and off the main roads on our way to the Miller Road Big K stop-and-rob. We needed smokes, snacks, and Coke to cut the rum. The Coke made it taste better and made the evening last longer. We had three hours of game time before we had to get back to school for Aaron's mom to pick us up.

The Big K on Miller was pretty run down, even for the Creek. The security cameras inside and outside were the most valuable things attached to the store. The three of us walked in together and the fat middle-aged woman behind the counter stared us down. We decided to forgo any food. Aaron grabbed a liter of Coke, and we headed to the front. I loudly spilled a bunch of change onto the counter, most of which fell on the floor behind. Once the woman's head disappeared under the counter, Brody snatched a pack of Marlboros from behind her, then buried them quickly inside his hooded sweatshirt. By the time the woman looked up, Brody was out the door. Aaron grabbed the Coke, and we started to leave.

"Here," the woman said as she held out the receipt. "You gave me too much."

"Keep the change!" I yelled at her as I snatched the receipt. I laughed loudly at Brody's five-finger discount and at my strange ex-Dad defiance: let this woman count the change, not me.

Brody and Aaron were waiting in the area behind the store. Brody had the smokes buried in his pocket just in case the security camera was actually on and somebody was really watching. With a murder a week in the Flint area, I knew nobody would care about petty crime. We exchanged high fives all around, then started to head toward WindGate. I could see the dim light of the trailer park from a distance, but Aaron—who was leading—stopped in his tracks.

"What's wrong, dude?" Brody shouted.

"Shit, I'm not sure which way to go from here," Aaron said. "Sorry."

I looked in front of me: there were two paths converging in the woods. "Which one?"

"I don't know," Aaron mumbled, unused to leading. That was usually Brody's job, not his.

"Mick? You must be able to smell it from here," Brody said, then laughed.

I scratched my forehead, then pointed down the path to the left. "This way, I think."

We forged over fallen branches, the twigs snapping beneath us sounding like fire.

"Who is it?" A strange garbled voice yelled out, which startled us all.

"Look, it's the Scarecrow," Brody said, then pointed at the figure in the straw hat who must have been equally as surprised. He was running, or limping quickly, away from us.

"What's he doing here?" I asked no one in particular.

"Living," Aaron offered. I wasn't sure if it was a statement or a question.

"If you call it that," Brody said, then motioned for us to join him off the beaten path. Behind one of the trailers was a small storage shed with the door hanging off the hinge. We looked inside: there was a damp green sleeping bag, empty beer cans, and newspapers covering the cold ground. There was a small pile of bricks forming a makeshift fireplace or stove in the corner. The place reeked of piss, shit, and beer.

"My sister's got to get to work," Aaron said as he nudged me on my way.

"Work," I said, then winked at Brody. Brody laughed while Aaron tried not to. Unlike the night before when he was pretty talkative, Aaron seemed sunk into himself. Brooding.

Aaron's sister was standing in front of the trailer, looking twenty shades of pissed off. She waved us in; Aaron didn't say anything as she handed him a paper bag. Aaron reached into his pocket, but Brody stopped him with a shout, barely heard over the blaring TV.

"Hey, Aaron, loan me twenty bucks," Brody said, then slapped Aaron on his shoulder.

"What?" Aaron looked confused, while his sister's overly made-up face didn't hide her scorn.

"Sure." Aaron took the money intended for his sister and handed it to Brody.

"I'm buying! Drinks on me!" Brody shouted, then handed the twenty to Aaron's sister.

"Real funny," Aaron's sister, Tonya, said as she reached out her hand to take the money from Brody, but I interrupted.

"My treat," I said. Aaron gave us the place, and Brody gave us a center, so I could pay with my unused homecoming funds. In our threesome, their roles were clear; I was still searching for mine.

"Dude, no way," Brody said, but I ignored him and handed her the money.

"What, no receipt?" I mumbled as Tonya took the cash and I took the bag. She handed me back a five and one icy stare when I counted the change.

"You be gone by the time I get home," she said. I wondered how she could move her mouth wearing so much frosted blue lipstick and how she could blink with the mountain of matching blue eye shadow covering her mostly dead blue eyes. She pulled out a smoke and then stuffed the twenty into her small black purse. The purse matched the long leather black jacket and short leather skirt she wore, but not the spiky red heels or scarlet fishnets.

"Need a light?" I asked.

"Thanks," she replied. My hand shook a little when I sparked the flint to fire up her smoke. Truth was, Aaron's sister's in-your-face-skank look more scared than excited me.

"We've got to get back to school by ten," Aaron said.

"And if you get caught, I don't know nothin' about this," she said. "I'm dead serious."

"Sure thing, Tonya," Aaron mumbled.

"And don't mess up the place," she said. I laughed first, Brody laughed loudest, and Aaron for the first time that night cracked a smile. "Assholes!"

"Sorry, Tonya," Aaron said. Brody tossed aside a pile of clothes on the stained brown carpet to make a place for himself on the sofa. He muted the TV as he surfed channels.

"Maybe I'll tell Mom about this," she fired back, smoke shooting out of her pierced nose. "Maybe your Friday night fun dries up. You think that's funny?"

"Sorry," I mumbled while Brody added a concurring grunt from the other room.

"Next time, price goes up," she said, then opened the door to leave. "How funny is that?"

Aaron didn't say anything as she slammed the door so hard the trailer seemed to shake. The booming music from her beat-up SUV started up almost immediately.

"Your sister's something!" Brody shouted as we heard the SUV pull away.

"You got something to say, Brody?" Aaron said, looking embarrassed, sounding angry.

"He's just busting you," I said, trying to act the peacemaker. "It's all good."

"I know, but you know how it is," Aaron said to me, as he handed me the Coke.

"How what is?"

"You gotta protect the women in your life, right?" Aaron said, and I smiled.

"I guess." I started toward the kitchen. As I thought about Aaron's comment, I felt a little guilty about lying to my mom, but I figured I'm really just doing what Aaron just said: protecting her from the truth of my life.

In the kitchen, I found three clean glasses that I filled with ice.

"Hurry up, Mick, thirsty men over here!" Brody shouted from the living room. It sounded like a college football game was blaring on the TV. I laughed. Now I could tell my mom a truth about what we did tonight: *just watched a football game.*

I brought the glasses back into the living room, then opened up both the Coke and the rum. I let the smell of rum linger in my nose before I filled the glasses half full with Bacardi. I put Coke in my glass and Aaron's, but Brody waved it away. With my first small sip, the rum tickled the top of my mouth, then began it's trip through my blood-stream.

I sat down next to Brody, deep in thought. This was a once-a-week thing, I told myself. I suspected Brody would get drunk every night if he could. If every day was like to-day, I thought, then I would second the rum-and-Coke solu-tion. Except neither of us could afford it.

"Happy Friday!" Brody shouted, then raised his glass

into the air. Aaron just grunted. He seemed distracted and detached.

"What's happy about it?" I grumbled as I thought how I'd rather have my lips wrapped around Whitney's or Nicole's lips than a glass, which I was working on emptying.

"Mick, she ain't worth it," Brody said, then raised his glass high again. "Here's to best friends!"

"To friends," Aaron said as he raised his glass. I set down my glass, pulled out my lighter, flicked it, and let the friendship flame burn.

"Mick wants to tap some ass, right?" Brody said.

"I'm trying, man, I'm trying," I said, knowing how much I've practiced if and when the day should ever come. I thought right then that I'd give ten years of my life for ten minutes with Whitney, ten more days with Nicole, or to wipe away my one encounter with Roxanne.

"Seems our man Aaron is the only one getting himself some," Brody said as he slapped Aaron's knee. "Maybe one day we'll meet her, what do you think?"

"Maybe," Aaron shrugged as Brody reached for the bottle. While the faraway look in his eyes remained, Aaron joined the party at last as Brody poured more rum into his glass.

The conversation stopped, stalled, and fired in a hundred directions over the next hour: Brody told stories, Aaron alternated between laughing loudly and pulling at his hair silently, while I just tried to keep up. By the half time of the TV game was over, more than half the rum-and-Coke solution to any problem had vanished. During half time, we moved over to a table in the kitchen. Brody sent Aaron on a mission to find some cards so we could play poker.

Over the roar of the TV, I thought about this night as a science experiment: the effect of alcohol on adolescent males. Subject Aaron sunk even deeper into himself, like a black hole imploding. Subject Brody got louder, more aggressive, like a superfuckingnova exploding into the dark night sky. Subject Mick needed more testing, for his reactions are the most inconsistent; his energy was in flux like a comet without a clear path.

"I found the cards," Aaron said, then tossed a deck on the table.

"Wanna play the bank, ATM?" Brody said, but I winced. I knew Brody was drunk since ATM was a behind-the-back, not an in-your-face nickname for a good friend.

"Right," Aaron mumbled while I shot Brody a nasty look. I knew Aaron didn't like this nickname, but he laughed anyway.

"Dude, don't call Aaron that," I said. Brody's face washed out, like a wave of sobriety splashed over him. Not because he felt guilty about his words, but because he was surprised I corrected him.

"Just kidding, ATM, you know that," Brody said. Aaron nodded, and I relaxed, while Brody shuffled the cards. Another half an hour got sucked up as we smoked, drank, and played poker. I was an even worse poker player than I was a pool player, although the problem was the same: hand-eye coordination. Although in poker, it was too much hand-eye coordination, for whenever I had a good hand, I couldn't help but smile. I've tried to put on that poker face, but I'm just not wired that way. I can lie to Mom, ex-Dad, and teachers about just about anything, but once the cards get dealt, I can't keep the hand I'm holding secret.

The poker made me feel restless, as much as Brody's shouting and Aaron's silence made me feel nervous. I told Brody to deal me out. I said I was going to take a piss, but truth was, I just needed to get away for a few minutes. The rum was buzzing my head and churning my stomach. I started to walk around the trailer to kill time and my dark thoughts.

I passed by the bathroom and stepped into the bedroom. Just inside the room was a crowded dresser. It was covered with makeup, overflowing ashtrays, and dusty framed photos. One picture was of a family: there was Aaron, his sister, and his mom. Aaron looked to be about nine or ten, so it's a picture from before Aaron moved into our neighborhood. But there were two other people in the picture: an older man who looked like Aaron—it had to be his dad—and there was another guy, maybe an older brother. A brother Aaron had never mentioned; a dad that Aaron told us died when he was five. A death the three of us drank to the evening before. A death that bonded Brody and Aaron.

"Aaron, I thought your dad died when you were five?" I said as I walked back into the living room, the picture in hand. "I mean, that's what we were remembering last night, right?"

"What?" Aaron stared at me. His eyes were blurry;

maybe because Aaron spoke the least, he drank the most. "Why are you asking me about my dad?"

"Mick, what's your problem?" Brody sounded agitated.

"Who is this?" I held up the picture, pointed to the father figure, and then put the photo in front of Aaron like a cop handling evidence. I sat back down at the table waiting for Aaron to speak.

"Look—you see—" Aaron stumbled over his words as Brody examined the picture.

"Dude, what's going on?" Brody's anger flashed. "We drank to his memory last night."

Aaron was silent for a long time, filling the vacuum by filling up all of our glasses, then finally he said, "Well, he's gone, just not by accident, that's all."

"What do you mean?" I followed up. I felt like some TV show detective.

"Guys, just let it alone," Aaron said, and then shuffled the cards.

"You can't lie to your friends, Aaron," I said, taking time to stress each word of the sentence. "If you can't tell your friends the truth, then you can't tell anyone."

"You lied about this!" Brody shouted. Aaron and Brody's shared past losses at the hands of auto accidents bonded them, but I wondered if Aaron knew Brody's whole story.

Aaron paused, emptied his glass, and then spoke. "He's in Huntsville."

"What's that?" Brody asked. There was no breeze whipping through the trailer, but I felt a chill. I'd heard about

Huntsville last year in current events class when we talked about the death penalty.

"Huntsville's a prison in Texas," Aaron said with a sigh. I thought the sigh sounded a little like ex-Dad's, maybe with the same motive. Maybe Aaron was impatient with himself for lying to his best friends for the past three years.

"Huntsville," I repeated, then motioned for the rum. The cards were on the table and all eyes were on Aaron. Aaron hated the attention, but we'd called and he had to show.

"Aaron, what the hell are you talking about?" Brody slammed his fist on the table.

"Guys, I don't want to talk about it, okay?" Aaron said, eyes downcast.

"I don't care what you want!" Brody shouted while I continued my stare. "Spill it!"

"Guys, do you know what my first real memory of my dad is?" Aaron asked, his voice cracked. "When I was like, three, he must have got some money someplace because we went in to Houston to watch *Sesame Street Live,* one of those stage shows. And I remember him buying us cotton candy, and buying himself beer after beer. He's there with his kids at a *Sesame Street* show getting drunk. He couldn't control himself, that's all you need to know."

"You lied to us," I said. Brody nodded in approval.

Aaron took a drink, then a deep breath. He was wildly twisting his hair with his fingers. "One night, he came home stinking drunk. It must have been when he was out of work, which was most of the time. Whatever was wrong was our fault. He had this belt, this big cowboy belt."

"Cowboy belt?" I asked.

"I was born in Texas, a place called League City, just outside of Houston," Aaron continued. "My parents moved there from Michigan after my dad got laid off from GM. I guess he found work there for a while. Something must have happened to his job, because I remember when I was real young sleeping in the car. Then he'd get work, things would be okay for a while, then it would all fall apart again. It was like living in a house of straw."

"Man, that's messed up," I muttered.

"So, when I was about eight, he'd been laid off again and just came home stinking drunk. He took that belt, with that big cowboy belt buckle, and he started on my mom. Called her a whore and a bunch of other stuff. Just beat the shit out of her, not the first time, but worse than usual. I started yelling loud."

"Why did he do that?" I asked.

"Why do you think? He was drunk, angry, and out of control."

"What happened?" I asked between drinks. Brody still wasn't talking. He bounced the deck of cards forcefully in his hand, making the table shake like an earthquake.

"Well, then my older brother, Stan—he was ten—tells my dad to knock it off. Well, that just sets my dad off even more."

"Aaron, you have an older brother?" I asked.

There was a moment of silence before Aaron replied in a whisper, "I don't anymore."

"Dude, I'm sorry," I said, even though I knew nothing I could say would really matter.

"Stan told him to stop, screamed at him, and then my

dad said—and I'll never forget the words or how he said them—he slurred, 'What are you gonna do about it?' and then laughed. Stan was a little guy, but he did something. He tried to grab the belt out of my dad's hand."

Aaron took a drink. I noticed his hand was shaking as much as his voice and the table.

"It didn't take much. He hit him once hard across the face with the belt. It was like his face exploded. I couldn't do anything. Stan started crying and my dad is screaming for him to stop, but he can't because he's so scared and so hurt. My dad takes the belt and wraps it around his throat. He went limp within a minute."

"Aaron, I'm so sorry." I felt useless, and thirsty as I reached for the half-empty fifth.

"Stan wasn't a big kid; so that first shot knocked him down. Then the little shit cried, rather than just taking it. He'd beat us all before but not like this. If you cried, it made him madder, so I learned not to cry. I think the tears just reminded him what he was doing, which made him feel worse, which made him hit more. Anyway, that's what one of the counselors told us one time."

"He didn't come back after you?" I asked.

"He didn't get a chance," Aaron said. "My mom was like in shock, just kind of not moving. After he choked Stan, then he started toward my sister. She was in the corner of the room, crying, shaking, totally trapped. He was waving the belt over his head. He must have lost sight of me for a second because I ran into the kitchen and grabbed the phone off the wall."

Brody continued to bounce the cards, while I pushed Aaron to continue. "The phone?"

"I wish now I would have grabbed a knife and rammed it into his heart. I wish I would have grabbed a pan or something and crashed it into his skull, but I was too little, too scared."

"So you called the police?" I asked.

"I got as far as dialing 9, then 1, and then he caught me. He stared me down. Told me to put the phone down or else. He had blood all over his face, but I knew it wasn't his blood."

"No way," Brody slurred. His mouth rejoined the conversation. His eyes had never left.

"He grabbed my arm, ripped it out of the socket, but I'd already pushed the last 1." Aaron started to cry. "I heard the voice say, 'What is your emergency?' but not much more. My sister had jumped on my dad's back and was trying to choke him, and then I dove at his legs. It was pretty loud, so I think the 911 people knew something was wrong. Really, really wrong."

"Did the police come?" I asked.

"It was too late. Stan was dead and Dad was gone," Aaron said. I noticed his fingers had pulled more twisted hair from his head. "We didn't need police. We needed a body bag."

"They caught him, right?" Brody chimed in.

"Yeah, and that bastard fought to the end. He wouldn't confess to what he did. He wouldn't admit to anything, so there was this trial, and I had to testify against my dad."

"Were you scared?" I asked, as I flashed back on my own fear of truth telling.

"Dude, I was shitless. I remember I was wearing these gray pants and my grandmother helped me put on a tie, a red tie." Aaron spoke clearly as if he were describing a scene before him, not behind him. "And the one lawyer, the prosecutor, asked me what happened. And I told them everything, but it was hard. A lot harder than this because my dad was like twenty feet away, sitting there staring at me, just like he did in the kitchen the night he killed my brother. I had to sit there and say the words that sent my dad to prison. I've never ever forgotten that."

"And so you guys moved here?" I asked.

"After it was over, Mom moved us up here because we couldn't live in Texas anymore. She grew up in Flint and her sister lives here. She found a job, and then met my stepdad."

"You ever see your dad again?" Brody asked, then motioned for the rum.

"No, not once, although I hope to one day," Aaron said. His eyes were wet with tears and terror. "But it won't be soon because he's on death row and his number's coming up."

"Then when?" Brody said, then took another rum-only drink.

"Not in this life, but in another," Aaron said. "I'll find his sorry ass in the fiery furnaces of hell, and then I'll get my revenge. This time I won't be eight. This time I won't back away."

We were all silent as we passed the bottle of rum around,

the liter of Coke mostly untouched. The table was littered with Aaron's hair, tears, and truth.

"Your mom should have left him," I said, breaking the silence. "None of this would have happened, if she'd just left him."

"And do what? A high school dropout with no job, no money, and three kids to feed. Where was she going to go?" Aaron asked.

"What about calling the police?" I asked.

"She'd done that. Nothing happened. Maybe my dad would spend the night in jail, but that was it."

"But still." I couldn't find the right words, so I tipped the bottle again.

"This isn't a spanking for spilling a glass of milk, dudes, this was a massacre. The counselor said my father by that time so hated his life that he felt trapped and needed to strike out against everything in it." Aaron's words were loud and clear even if his voice had started to slur.

"The bastard should have just killed himself!" Brody shouted.

"But he couldn't," Aaron replied.

"Why?" I asked, then took a drink straight from the bottle.

"Because he was weak, because he was a piece of shit. People who are weak get the shit that's coming to them if you ask me," Aaron said, then stood up. He slowly looked around the room, then tipped over the table. The cards and our glasses flew all over the floor.

"Aaron, man, relax," Brody said. I had to hold in a laugh at the idea of Brody as the voice of calm. Brody was an

F-five tornado, but Aaron's winds were whipping up wildly. When I stood up quickly I realized that during Aaron's story we'd all been drinking a lot. I took one more quick swig, and then set the Bacardi bottle on the floor. I started to pick up the cards, but when I bent over, the the liquid making its way down my throat didn't have enough force to stop the heaving energy of the contents of my stomach from making its way up. I bolted from the living room, slid into the bathroom, and had perfect aim as I threw up into the toilet.

"I just heard his lung come up!" Brody shouted from the other room. It was funny, but I didn't laugh. I was too busy trying to catch my breath and clear the remnants of vomit from around my mouth. Even as the salty spit collected in my throat, I pledged this would be my last Friday night drinking with Brody and Aaron. This wasn't a road I wanted to stagger down again.

"You okay?" Aaron asked as I made my way back into the living room.

But before I could answer, Brody shouted, "Mick, you stupid clumsy motherfucker!"

"What did I do?" I asked. I wiped off my mouth, then saw the rum spilled on the dirty carpet, which had sucked up the stain. The bottle was now almost empty.

"You spilled it, man, it's all gone," Brody said as he slammed his fists into his legs.

"I'm sorry. I screwed up," I offered. My voice was a mix of embarrassment and anger.

"What now?" Aaron asked.

"You'd better figure something out," Brody said, then

poked me hard in the shoulder with his right hand. "This is your fucking fault. You cheated me out of my drunk, dude."

Looking into Brody's angry eyes and Aaron's sad face, I knew I'd better come up with a way to save the night I'd ruined. I thought for a moment, then said, "the Scarecrow."

"What about him?" Brody's voice was finally down to his normal loud level.

"Let's get him to buy us something else to drink." Even as I said it, I realized I was too drunk. But I'd screwed things up with my friends, and it was my job to make things right.

"I'm sure if we offer him a few bucks—" Aaron started to say.

But Brody cut him off. "Offer him beer instead."

I nodded, then walked toward the kitchen and grabbed some paper towels. I soaked up the stain, trying to hide the evidence. Aaron started picking up the mess he'd made on the floor, while Brody went to the bathroom. The room was totally silent, still, and calm. After we cleaned up, we headed out toward the place where we'd seen the Scarecrow earlier.

When we got to the rundown little shack, Brody cupped his hands, winked at me, then yelled, "Come out come out wherever you are!" I faked a laugh for Brody's sake, but what I really wanted to do was open my mouth and say, *Let's call it a night. We don't need to do this.*

"Who is it?" A voice emerged from behind the heavy growth of weeds and shrubs.

"You want some beer?" Aaron said, then took a step closer. "Mister, come talk to us."

"We ain't gonna hurt you," Brody promised.

The wind kicked up as the Scarecrow emerged from behind the shrubs. From even a few feet away, I could smell the beer on his breath and the stink of the piss that stained his pants. His hat was pulled almost over his eyes; his mouth and face were covered in sores. "What do you want?" His voice was rough and tough, like the bricks that lined his hovel.

I took a step forward. "Hey, go buy us some beer and you can keep some."

"How many?" the Scarecrow asked.

"Buy us a twelve-pack and we'll give you two," I told him.

"Four," the Scarecrow responded.

"Fuck you!" Brody shouted.

"Two," the Scarecrow said immediately.

"Get us Miller High Life, longnecks." Brody barked out the beer order like some TV drill sergeant. The Scarecrow grunted and held out his hand. My heart sank when I saw the skin on his right hand. It was red and raw, like it had been burned. I handed the guy a twenty, then we followed him in silence for the short walk to the Big K Market. The Scarecrow went inside while we waited behind the store under the buzzing neon light and silent security camera.

"How do you think this happened to him?" I asked Brody and Aaron.

"What?" Brody replied.

"The Scarecrow, how do you think he got like this?" I asked.

"Who knows?" Brody replied. "Who cares?"

"You sound like ex-Dad," I joked, but nobody was laughing anymore about anything.

"To fathers," Brody said, then made a mock toast, which I didn't join.

"To dead dads," Aaron added. "May they rot in peace."

"Where the fuck is he?" Brody slapped his right hand against his left bicep. "Dude, I think the Scarecrow ripped us all off. Stupid worthless drunk."

"Stupid worthless drunk," Aaron repeated.

I looked up at the security camera. If it had infrared sensors, the images of the three of us would be screaming, bloodred blotches of anger, impatience, and resentment. I felt a sudden urge to change the tone of the evening, which had taken a sharp turn onto a dark road.

"We're here live with Brody Warren, former star of the Swartz Creek Dragons football team," I said, waving Brody over to come stand next to me, then holding my hand in front of me.

Aaron cupped his hands to make a sound like the roar of a crowd. Brody waved to the security camera and pretended to sign autographs as he walked over to me.

"Brody, how do you think the team is going to do this year without you?" I asked.

"They suck," Brody said, then laughed.

"And that's because you're not on the team?" I said.

"Totally," Brody replied. "Most of the guys are losers, cheaters, and whiners."

"To what do you attribute your success?" I asked.

"Rum, Coke, and good friends," Brody said, then slapped me hard on the back.

I laughed, then looked straight into the camera. "Anyone you want to say hello to?"

"Here's a shout-out to my brothers and my mom," Brody shouted, then raised his fingers in the "we're number one" pose. "I'm going to Disney World!"

"It has been a pleasure interviewing you," I said as I noticed the Scarecrow walking toward us slowly. It looked like the bag he was carrying weighed more than he did.

"The pleasure has been all yours," Brody said, then we all laughed.

"Here," the Scarecrow said, handing me the change: the bills and coins mixed with the receipt, which I stuffed in my pocket. He then handed Brody a brown bag containing a twelve-pack of Miller High Life longnecks.

"Deal." Brody took out two of the beers and handed them to the Scarecrow.

"Thanks," the Scarecrow mumbled, then headed back into the woods.

None of us felt like walking back to Aaron's sister's, so we found a small clearing not too far from the Big K. We sat on the ground, and Brody opened the brown bag, pulling out a beer for each of us. I wasn't really paying much attention as Aaron started asking Brody questions about football, no doubt so we wouldn't talk about his lies anymore. I sipped my beer in the cool of the evening, holding it in my left hand. I put my right hand in my pocket and pulled out the money the Scarecrow had handed back to me. I felt the beer freeze the back of my throat when I did something ex-Dad put in my DNA: I counted the change.

"He shortchanged me," I mumbled to no one in particular.

"What?" Brody looked up from his beer, which he'd emptied in three or four gulps.

"Never mind," I whispered, almost trying to pretend I'd never said anything at all.

"How much?" Brody asked, his volume cranked back up.

"Nothing, just two dollars," I answered, reluctantly.

"Motherfucker!" Brody shouted, then hurled the bottle against a tree.

The sound of the shattering glass seemed to awaken Aaron, who'd been lost in High Life and his own thoughts. "That's what drunks do," he said.

"It's not a big deal," I said, looking at the ground, toward the spot where Brody's feet had been. But he was gone: running into the woods. I shouted, "Brody, where are you going?"

But I knew: my heart raced as fast as my feet as I grabbed the bag with the beer, then chased after Brody, with Aaron just a step behind me.

"I'm sick of being cheated and ripped off!" Brody shouted over his shoulder. By the time we caught up with him, he was standing outside the Scarecrow's makeshift house.

"Let it go," I said, trying to catch my breath and calm Brody down, failing at both.

"Like that stupid bitch Mrs. Kirby!" Brody shouted. His long brown hair seemed wilder, his eyes unfocused, and his anger unhinged. "Everybody thinks they can take from me."

"Brody, let's go," I said as I reached out my right hand to pull him back.

"Fuck you!" Brody shouted at me, then knocked my hand away. I reached out again to grab his arm, but he pushed hard against my chest. I stumbled back while he charged inside the makeshift house with us in hot pursuit. "You cheated us, you motherfucker!"

The Scarecrow was leaning against the pile of bricks, slurping down one of the beers. "I didn't—" the Scarecrow started.

But Brody became a monster with no ears, just a mouth. "Don't sit there in your fucking filth and fucking lie to me!" he shouted, casting his large shadow over the Scarecrow.

"I'm not." The Scarecrow seemed stuck, so Brody kicked him into gear. While he didn't kick as hard as he'd kicked Garrett at the party, Brody landed his size twelve shoe into the Scarecrow's shoulder. The Scarecrow didn't move or make a sound; he just spat on the ground.

"I'm fucking sick and tired of being cheated by every-one!" Brody shouted.

The Scarecrow rubbed his shoulder, then let out a small, garbled laugh. "What are you gonna do about it?" Even if the words were slightly slurred, the meaning behind them was not.

In the time it takes to blink an eye or ruin a life, Aaron

reached behind the Scarecrow and grabbed one of the red bricks. There was a quick look of surprise on his face that vanished the second Aaron smashed the brick into his skull. Even a dull thud can produce an echo.

"Drunken loser!" Aaron shouted as he brought the brick down again on the Scarecrow's head. The Scarecrow fell back, blood spurting from the top of his head. He didn't scream, he just moaned. Rather than reaching for his injured head, he reached for his leg. From his sock, he pulled out a short knife, which he used to slice open Aaron's ankle.

"Aaron, stop it," I finally said, breaking through the paralysis of my throat, but Aaron didn't, wouldn't, or couldn't hear me. The Scarecrow held the knife in front of him pointing it at Aaron again, but Brody kicked him from behind. When he fell backward, Aaron landed another hard shot with the brick, this time in the throat. There was a strangled drowning sound as the Scarecrow spat up blood, most of which landed on Aaron's face. Brody started to stomp on the Scarecrow's prone body like he was on fire and Brody was trying to extinguish the flames.

Every sense was working overtime. I heard his last gasps in between the heavy breathing of Brody and Aaron. I heard the smack of shoe and brick on his body. As Aaron and Brody continued their savagery, I was paralyzed in the middle of a nightmare with no way to wake up.

. . .

Brody's eyes were almost as red as the blood staining Aaron's gray hoodie and sock. Aaron crawled off the Scarecrow, wrapped himself up like a ball on the ground next to the dead body, and started to rock back and forth. I couldn't tell if he was crying, laughing, or a little bit of both. I sat with my head between my legs, ready to throw up again. For a long while no one spoke through the death-filled air, until Aaron finally mumbled, "Mick, this is your fault."

"*My* fault," I said, trying to look anywhere except at the bloody heap next to Aaron.

"If you wouldn't have spilled the rum," Aaron said, his head between his knees as his hand applied pressure to his ankle.

"Shut up!" Brody screamed. "We're not going to do this!"

"Do what?" I asked.

"Point fingers," Brody said, then acted out the motion. "That doesn't help anything."

"What *are* we going to do?" Aaron mumbled.

"How the fuck should I know?" Brody shouted. "Mick, you need to figure this out."

I crawled over to the body, the dead body, for there was no pulse or breath. "I don't know, I guess we call the police and—" I started.

But Brody cut me off. "No police."

"But Aaron and you killed a—"

"Aaron didn't do anything, I didn't do anything, and you didn't do anything," Brody said as he reached over to the brown bag. He pulled out a beer, then rolled one over to me and one to Aaron. Brody took a drink, but this time there was no toast. "No one finds out."

"Besides, he was dead already," Aaron said. The beer remained unopened next to him. "You think if anybody cared about him, he'd be living like this? He's nothing. Trust me, we did him and anyone that knew him a favor, putting everyone out of their misery."

"Who would know if he was living or dead?" Brody asked me, almost in a whisper.

"We would," I said as I stared at the pile of rags, blood, bone, flesh, and skin.

"Dude, this doesn't leave here," Brody announced. I knew if he was close enough, he'd seal the deal with a slap of the arm or poke to the chest. "Nobody talks, right?"

I shook my head to agree, but doubt drowned me. "But what if?"

"What if what?" Aaron asked.

"What happens when somebody finds the body—I mean—what then?" I asked.

"Then they can't." Brody let his words hang there and waited for someone to finish.

"Can't what?" Aaron asked. When Brody didn't answer, I knew it was my place.

"Find the body," I said as Brody nodded in agreement. I finally realized what my role in this friendship was. I was supposed to be the smart one, the guy with the answers. Shit, were we in trouble.

I got up, took a last sip of beer, but left the bottle half full. Then I walked over to the prone bloody body of the Scarecrow and poured the beer on his bloody bashed-in face. I found some dry newspaper and stuffed it under his body.

Finally, I pulled the bone white lighter from my pocket. I offered it first to Aaron, then to Brody.

"You do it," Brody said, while staring me down. "It *is* your turn."

I listened to the sounds of Brody's and Aaron's footsteps as they shuffled back outside, leaving me alone with the stinking dead body and a foul deed in front of me. I heard crickets chirp and an airplane pass overhead. I imagined miles away the Dragons scoring a touchdown, sending the crowd into a frenzy of applause. Miles away women were shopping, laughing, and spending money as Mom turned on a smile to sell them more clothes they didn't need. Miles away men were drinking and leering as Aaron's sister shook her ass and took their money. I pretended I heard these sounds of the living, so I could pretend that I was miles away from the death in front of me. Pretended to hear laughter rather than the sound of the thumb on my shaking right hand flicking the lighter. Pretended to hear anything other than the almost silent crackling of the fire starting to burn the Scarecrow's body and send his soul up to heaven and my soul into a free fall straight to hell.

. . .

We returned quickly to Aaron's sister's trailer. Aaron found some men's clothes for us to change into. Aaron bandaged the cut on his ankle, and we wrapped our beer and blood-stained clothes in trash bags—including Brody's shoes—then threw them in the Dumpster at the other end of the trailer park. When we left via the front entrance of

WindGate, I thought I saw smoke through the trees and tasted ash sticking to the roof of my mouth.

As we walked quickly back toward school, the conversation was minimal: I wanted to talk about "it" but Brody's eyes screamed at me to be quiet, while Aaron looked like he was lost.

We arrived in the school parking lot just a few silent minutes before the buses started to pull up. A wave of red washed over us as the Dragon diehards climbed off the buses into waiting cars. I didn't see Whitney, Shelby, or Nicole, and I was amazed at how little they mattered to me. All I cared about was when and if the smell of smoke would ever leave my body.

Brody left us for a moment and walked across the lot. He chatted briefly with someone, ending the conversation with a slap on the back. When he returned, he said, "We lost twenty-seven to ten."

I wanted to say, *Brody, why are you telling me this? I never cared about football, but now, even less so. Brody, what are we going to do? This isn't a football game. Aaron, this isn't a video game. This is real.* But instead, I just gave him a puzzled look. We didn't talk again until Aaron's mother arrived. We quickly piled in so she wouldn't notice our ill-fitting clothes.

In the car, the conversation was minimal except for Brody speaking about the game. He repeated the score five times, due to anxiety or alcohol, maybe both. The short drive drove me nearly insane. It reminded me of that Poe story Mrs. Kirby had us read: "The Tell-Tale Heart," about a guy who killed somebody, then buried him under his floor. He confessed to the crime because he was driven insane by thinking he heard the beating of the dead guy's heart under the floor. Locked in the car, Aaron's mom had to hear my heart beating faster than normal. She had to see the sweat, even in my coatless state, dripping down my brow. She had to smell the smoke, not of cigarettes, but of something much worse.

Aaron's mother dropped me off, and Brody got out with me. She said good night and seemed to be waiting for a response. But before I could say anything, my words and thoughts were both drowned out by the sound of the only thing louder than the beating of my heart: the sound of a siren.

. . .

Brody waited until the scream of the siren faded before he spoke. "Relax, Mick," he said as he tamped his last cigarette up and down on his hand, before putting it behind his right ear.

"Brody, we—" I started, but stopped since there was nothing to say or think. Instead, I wondered why I'd never noticed all the cracks in the driveway. I focused on the cracks as they broke off into separate paths, then formed more cracks: all of them small, all of them connected.

"Look, we've done this before," Brody said.

"What do you mean?" I asked.

"Done stupid stuff, but we don't snitch on each other," Brody reminded me. "Like today with that paper. I could've said you wrote it, but I didn't. We've covered for Aaron, you've covered for me. Friends cover for each other. We can do this."

"Do what?"

"Not tell about this," Brody almost whispered. "Those sirens, that's probably a fire truck. There won't be anything left of the Scarecrow for them to find, and we can forget it happened."

"But on TV—" I started, thinking about every TV crime show I'd ever witnessed.

Brody laughed, but my mouth couldn't move in an upward direction. "This is fucking Swartz Creek, Mick, not New York or Vegas. I doubt there's a *CSI Flint.*"

"I guess."

"Nobody's going to know," Brody said in the tone of a teacher announcing a test. Brody moved from the driveway and sat on the lawn. He leaned back, resting on his elbows, and looked up into the night sky.

"But what if?" I asked.

"Besides, it was just the Scarecrow," Brody said, then grunted. Like he was unsure of the spin to put on the words. "I mean, Aaron was right. It's not like anybody's going to care."

I shrugged, but wanted to say, *Dude, he's still a person. Or rather, he* was *a person.*

"Don't be scared," Brody told me. I wasn't sure if it was a suggestion or an order.

"I'm not," I said, another step down what seemed like an endless road of lies.

"You can keep a secret; I know that," Brody said, then kind of half smiled. I scratched my head, then joined Brody sitting on the lawn, looking at the infinite sky rather than the equally infinite connection of cracks in the dull gray driveway. The siren had long vanished; the crickets in the air and cars out on the street took over again as the soundtrack for the late evening.

"Weird about Aaron's dad, huh?" Brody mumbled, like he didn't want to be heard.

I cracked my knuckles as my answer, knowing there was not much left to say. I was surprised by Aaron's story, but then not by his actions or Brody's. For us all, the Scarecrow was the last straw. I thought I knew Aaron; I was wrong. I thought I knew what Brody was capable of, but I was also wrong. The only question remaining as I looked up at the almost full moon, which looked like a cue ball shining white in the sky, was, What was I capable of doing?

Brody broke into my thoughts with a stiff slap to my leg. "I gotta get home."

I got up and dusted the grass stains off my borrowed pants.

"It's gonna be okay," Brody reminded me, and I nodded in agreement. I was too tired, too stressed, and too everything to say anything, or even think of things I wanted to say.

"Light me up!" Brody shouted as he pulled his last cigarette from behind his ear.

I buried my hand in my pocket and my heart raced. Every nerve cell in my body tingled; I wanted to scream and stomp my feet. Instead, I took a deep breath, feeling only acid in my lungs. I quickly turned my back on Brody and acted like I didn't hear him. I put my head down and sprinted into the house, leaving him alone in the darkness with his unlit smoke. There's no light because there's no lighter. The bone white lighter with my fingerprints all over it was on the ground next to the charred bones and melted skin of the Scarecrow.

Part Two

Sunday, November 14

9:30 a.m.

I was jolted awake by the ringing of the telephone. I took a quick glance at the clock wondering who would be calling me early on a Sunday morning. The phone felt heavy as I picked it up. I guessed maybe it was ex-Dad telling me one of those "work things" had come up, so he wouldn't be taking me to the Lions football game. I wouldn't be surprised by his broken promise; in fact, I almost expected constant disappointment from him.

"Hello." My rough morning voice croaked into the receiver.

"Have you seen the paper?" It was Brody.

"What paper?" I asked.

"The fucking *Flint Urinal,* what do you think?" Brody shouted through the phone.

"No, why?" I said, as I recalled how I used to enjoy reading the newspaper. I got hooked when Mr. Daunt made us study current events in social studies. But since that night, I couldn't bring myself to even glance at it. I was afraid of seeing my picture on the front page.

"There's an obituary," Brody said. He was struggling for words. "He had a name."

"Who?"

"The Scarecrow had a name," Brody answered. Before I could tell Brody I didn't want to know any more, he dropped it like a bag of bricks. "Edward Shreve."

There was silence on both ends of the phone, not mourning the death, but instead mourning the birth of Edward Shreve to both of us. He'd been the Scarecrow: not real, but a character without a true name. If he had a name, he was a person. If he was a person, then my name would have another word next to it: murderer.

"You know who that is?" Brody asked.

"It's the Scarecrow," I replied, wondering why Brody was acting so dense.

"No, dude, I think it's Cell Phone Girl's father," Brody whispered.

"What?"

"Her name is Lauren Shreve. The paper said he's from Swartz Creek and he had a daughter," Brody said, as I recalled that Cell Phone Girl had missed school on Friday.

More silence, except for the sound of me cracking my knuckles.

"Dude, do you think I should tell her?" Brody said softly.

"Are you crazy?" The thought raised me out of bed. I checked to see that the door was closed, but wondered if Mom was on the other end of the phone. "Are you fucking crazy?"

I listened closely; the *F* word would smoke her out if she was listening in without permission. Instead, there was just more silence.

"I know, I know," Brody repeated. "Don't worry, Mick, what happened dies with us."

I wanted to say, *I understand you wanting to tell someone. I can't bear this burden of knowing and not telling. But*

I know we can't change the past; we gotta protect our futures. Like you said, this dies with us. Yet, as each day passed since that night, I wondered if telling would enable me to sleep, eat, or breathe again. I couldn't speak of that night to anyone. We'd really only talked about it once. The next night, we'd got our stories together. No one ever suggested going to the police. No one spoke of the details. Our code of silence was complete.

"We can't talk about this over the phone," I offered. "Can you come over?"

"We're going to church in, like, five minutes," Brody replied.

"Stay away from confession," I joked, to no response.

"Dude, calm down," Brody replied, and I seethed in silence.

After a long pause, I asked, "What now?"

"You're the center of all this," Brody said aloud, which was what I guessed both he and Aaron had been thinking ever since that night. I wasn't just the center; I was the point of the triangle.

"Brody, listen, it was Aaron who—" I started.

Brody cut off me. "It was your idea to find the Scarecrow."

"But you were the one who—"

But Brody finished it. "Dude, it doesn't matter now. It's done." I thought how wrong Brody was: because it was done, now these questions mattered more. They're questions we've told ourselves we'll never answer: to our families, the police, a judge, or a jury. In my heart, the fear of being caught crushed the guilt of what I'd done every single time.

"Fine, I'll call Aaron," I said.

"When're you getting back from the game?" Brody asked. He tried to sound casual, like this was just another phone call. Like it was just another morning. Like nothing had changed.

"I don't know, around six," I said as I finally swung my feet onto the cold floor.

"Tell Aaron, we'll shoot some pool tonight, figure this out," Brody said.

"Fine." I decided to save my words. I needed to teach myself not to talk. I wouldn't say what I needed to, let alone what I wanted to, which was, *Brody, what is there to figure out? They found the body. They know who he is. If they figured out who he was, then they can figure out how he died. How he was murdered. Then they can figure out who did it. Then our lives are over, too.*

"I gotta go," Brody said hurriedly, not even saying good-bye before he hung up.

I slammed the phone down in frustration at Brody, Aaron, and myself. I crawled out of bed, then headed to the bathroom. My head ached, not from drinking since I've not touched a drop since that night, but from lack of sleep. Once I fell asleep, I was fine, but I'd seen too many two in the mornings these past nights. When I woke up in the morning, I lay in the bed, anxiety like a heavy wet blanket I couldn't shake off.

I'd barely made it to school each day. I pretended to care about classes. I couldn't see the world in front of me: my vision was clouded with doubt and dread. I was in my personal hell, nothing but waiting. Just feeling utterly and totally helpless to change a thing.

I heard Mom in the kitchen, so I needed to join her and act normal. I wondered if she could see the battle that raged in me. Every day I had fought, and every day I had beat, the urge to return: I wanted to return to the scene of the crime, not to relive the horror and not to relieve my guilt, but to try to retrieve the lighter. But every day after school, I thought about getting off the bus at WindGate and getting back my life that was still buried in the ashes. That shadow of doubt, a huge, dark, thundering, hovering mass of suspicion, hung over me more than anything—more than the guilt, more than the regret—perhaps matched only by fear. Fear that I would break and talk, and doubt that both Aaron and Brody would stay silent. Aaron, I didn't trust: Aaron kept his true history from Brody and me. If you lied about one thing, you would lie about anything. I knew Aaron was a survivor. As I dialed his number, I wondered if that instinct would trump all others, even friendship.

"Hello?" Aaron's mom's voice sounded odd to me.

"It's Mick. Is Aaron there?" I pulled out my polite talking-to-adults voice.

"He's still asleep," she replied. "Do you want me to wake him up? Is it important?"

I paused. Every question was a trap. If I said it was important, then she would want to know why. That would force another lie. If I lied again, then I would need to remember it. Carrying the burden of falsehood was breaking my back. "Just have him call me, okay?"

"Well, he should probably be up by now, anyway; just a moment," Aaron's mom said and the line went silent. I wanted to say, *Mrs. Bishop, I know all about what happened with your son and your husband. I'm really sorry.* But as the words formed in my head, they were burned away by thoughts of a possible conversation between Brody and Cell Phone Girl: *Hey, I'm really sorry to hear about your dad. How did I know? Umm, you see . . .*

"Mick?" Aaron said softly.

"Hey, Brody called and said you should look at the paper," I told him. As Aaron considered what I said, I realized Brody was right: I was both the center and the point. While I didn't lift a finger to help or hinder, I was the one who lit the spark that started and ended it.

"Why?" Aaron said after a pause.

"Look in the obituaries," I answered. "Look under the name Shreve."

"Who?"

Even though I knew Mom couldn't hear, I whispered anyway, "The Scarecrow."

"So what?"

"So, I don't know. It creeps me out to know he had a name, a life, a family," I said.

"He's still dead," Aaron replied. "Dead is dead."

"But, man, what we did to him," I said as I struggled to find small words to wrap around my almost overwhelming feeling of remorse. I understood why Brody wanted to talk to the Scarecrow's daughter. I understood Brody wanting to say "I'm sorry" to someone because if I could say "I'm sorry," then someone could forgive me; if someone could forgive me, then I could stop feeling the guilt, the shame, the regret, and the dread that drove my days and nights.

"It's done, spilled milk," Aaron said flatly, but something spiked in me. The little we had talked about it, Aaron had never once expressed regret, only the fear of getting caught.

"Brody wants to get together tonight. We'll come by, okay?" The words rushed out of me.

"Fine," he said.

"You haven't told anyone, have you?" I said slowly, ashamed for asking but unable to stop myself.

"Have you?" Aaron replied.

"Who am I going to tell?" I said sharply. Telling ex-Dad was out of the question. I couldn't tell Mom either. It would crush her to know I could do something so horrible. But if I had told her, I knew she would protect me somehow. Mom's maternal instincts, I guessed, would be stronger than any notion of law, order, or justice.

"Well, I'm not talking," Aaron said. "What time are you coming over?"

"Six, maybe a little later."

"See you two then," Aaron said, then hung up the phone. In the white noise of the dial tone, I wondered why Aaron said "you two." I felt the urge to find my geometry book from last year. I was caught in a triangle of fate. What if Aaron and Brody were talking to each other without me? What if Brody really believed it was my fault and persuaded Aaron to believe likewise? The connections between Brody and me were stronger than those between Aaron and Brody, and me and Aaron. Maybe Aaron knew that and assumed Brody and I would team up. Maybe Brody thought that Aaron and I would team up against him. I drew triangles in my head as I started toward the kitchen. I thought about the shapes, sizes, and names, but in all of them, I was the point.

Mom sat in her usual spot curled up next to the heat vent as I stumbled into the kitchen. I could tell from the way she looked at me that she wanted to talk, which was never good for me.

"Good morning, Mom," I said, trying to break her icy stare.

"You feeling okay, Mick?" she replied lightning fast. "Is something wrong?"

I grunted, reaching for a cereal box. I avoided another lie by not answering the question.

"Mick, is there something you need to tell me? You seem distracted lately," she said.

I didn't answer out loud, only with the sound of the beating of my telltale heart.

"So, how was homecoming?" she asked. I wondered if she noticed me say "shit" under my breath. "Don't you have any pictures?"

I knew I was trapped in this lie. All week, I'd played along, even letting her buy me a new suit. Then last night, I'd told her more lies about my imaginary date. I'd actually hung out with Aaron and Brody. Not drinking, certainly not talking about the Scarecrow. That truth remained buried, but Mom had me busted. It was a matter of getting out with the least damage.

"You didn't go to homecoming, did you?" Mom said, then took a deep drag on her Kool.

I just stared at my empty bowl, not wanting to lie again, not ready to tell the truth.

Mom sighed as she expelled the smoke. "You're turning out just like your father." The tone in her voice slapped my face, but didn't dislodge my tongue from the back of my throat.

"Mick, how can you lie to me like that?" Her voice sounded beyond sad, almost lost.

"Mom, I . . ." But I faded out, like some sound disappearing off into the distance.

She shook her head. "Mick, didn't your father's example teach you anything?" I filled up my bowl, then leaned against the kitchen counter. I was unable to stand up straight.

"It's one thing to take money from me, but to lie to me, Mick, that's worse."

"I know, Mom," I finally said.

"Mick, say the words." She raised her voice but remained seated.

"I'm sorry," I mumbled.

"For what?" she asked. "It's not enough, Mick, to say you're sorry, you have to admit responsibility. You have to say the words. Don't be like your father, be a man. Admit it."

I stirred the cereal in my bowl, matching the churning in my stomach.

"Mick, show me you're becoming a man. Show me you're a better man than your—"

"Mom, I'm sorry I lied to you about homecoming," I confessed.

"What did you do with the money I gave you? I know your father gave you money, too."

"Spent it on stuff," I mumbled. I'd been wrong about my parents not talking. I'd trusted in their hatred of each other, but they'd betrayed me by speaking to each other, at least about me.

She shook her head like it weighed two thousand pounds. "Mick, this is very sad."

"You're not going to tell Dad that I got money from you, too, are you?"

"No, Mick, I won't tell him, I'll leave that to you," she said, then actually smiled.

"What are you smiling about?" I asked.

"I amaze myself," she said, then laughed. "When he asked me if I'd given you money for homecoming, too, I just avoided the question. I didn't lie to him, but I didn't tell him the truth. That's up to you."

"Okay," I said, knowing that telling the truth wasn't really going to bring any good to anyone.

"But if he pushed me, I probably would have lied to protect you, Mick. I guess my instinct is to do anything to protect you. You'll understand when you're a parent."

"Anything?" I asked. She nodded, confirming both her love and her powerlessness.

"A mother would do anything to protect her child," she said.

I wanted to ask her, *How can you protect me from the*

things I've already done? I finished my cereal as she finished her smoke. Before I could respond, she'd picked up her purse and left by the back door. She never stayed to see ex-Dad when he picked me up.

I saw the *Flint Journal* on the kitchen counter. I walked around it like it was a dead animal. I didn't need to read the words to make it more real than it already was, but I couldn't resist. Sometimes when I tried so hard to be strong, it only proved how weak I was.

OBITUARIES

Edward Shreve, 39, of Swartz Creek, died Friday, November 5, in a fire at his temporary residence.

He was the son of the late Floyd and Anna Shreve and a graduate of Flint Northern High School.

Shreve was previously employed as a skilled tradesman at the General Motors parts division in Swartz Creek.

Shreve is survived by his daughter, Lauren Shreve, and ex-wife, Marybeth Shreve, of Swartz Creek. Also surviving are two sisters, Alice Westlake of Minneapolis, Minnesota, and Mary Kramer of Houston, Texas; a brother, Bradley Shreve, and his wife, Margie, of Mission, Kansas; and several nieces and nephews.

The family suggests donations to the Eastern Michigan Food Bank in lieu of flowers. There will be a memorial service for family only at Kelly Funeral Home on Calkins Road in Swartz Creek.

I put down the paper, then ran into my bedroom all the while telling myself, *This isn't happening to me.* In bed, I so badly wanted to sleep, but rest had vanished with the Scarecrow's life. To sleep was to dream, but I didn't have room for dreams, just for nightmares.

The knock at the front door stirred my stress like witches at a boiling cauldron. I looked out the window to see if it was the police. Every knock at the door or ring of the phone caused that reaction. But it was only ex-Dad. I pulled it together and stumbled toward the door.

"Are you ready to go?" ex-Dad said as the bright winter sun almost blinded me when I opened the door. It wasn't a gust of wind that made the next sound, but ex-Dad's normal condition of impatience. He sighed, then added, "Mick, get dressed already."

I looked at the clothes that were disappointing ex-Dad: my *Dark Side of the Moon* T-shirt and blue jeans. "Fine," I snapped, and left him standing behind the slammed door. Per Mom's instructions, ex-Dad wasn't allowed in the house. I found that rule both mean and meaningful.

I went back to my room, and found tan slacks and a white shirt on the closet floor. As I rushed to get redressed, I imagined ex-Dad's foot tapping with impatience on the front stoop. Half of me wanted to take a long time to make him wait. The other half, the stronger half, hurried in some instinctive desire not to upset my father. As I buttoned up my one dress shirt, I stared into the mirror, thinking about Mom, who worked so hard to make my life better, thinking about all the things ex-Dad had done to make my life worse. The mirror reflected a truth I could no longer avoid. The one who loved me least was the one I would probably do anything to please. "That's better," ex-Dad said when I returned.

I nodded, then grabbed my winter coat even though it wouldn't warm the chill in my bones, which seemed infinite.

"Great day for football!" ex-Dad said as we walked toward his silver Tahoe parked in the dull gray, cracked driveway. I kept my head down, mouth closed, and got in.

"Help yourself," ex-Dad said as he pointed at a box of a donuts. There were two missing from the box and powdered sugar on the steering wheel. Last time we were together, he told me he was on a diet. By the time I finished my first one—the rush of sugar making me feel momentarily groggy—we were at the entrance to the expressway.

"I think the Lions are going to win today, yes sir," ex-Dad said.

"Maybe," I said, killing time and filling in the space in his sports monologue.

"Here's the problem with the Lions this year, if you ask me." And then he began his review of the offense, defense, special teams, etc. As ex-Dad rattled on, my mind was looking for a place to land. Not even the distracting detailed anti-Lions diatribe in my ear could move my mind from the Scarecrow. It was like my head was a TV, but no matter what button I pressed on the remote, there was only one show and it was in endless reruns.

As we drove to Detroit, I saw a billboard for a Chico's. It made me sad as I thought about the life Mom lived compared to the one she was promised by ex-Dad. Exhausted from lack of sleep, and desperate to talk about something that would distract me from my own mistakes, I interrupted ex-Dad's commentary on the Lion's running game, to ask him about something I had needed to know for a long time. "Why did you do it?"

"Do what?"

"Cheat on Mom," I said. My words set off a huge sigh, followed by a wall of silence. I wanted to understand ex-Dad so I could understand myself. After watching Brody self-destruct like his father and after seeing the violence bottled up in Aaron, I wondered if, like them, my future was determined for me by my father's actions.

"Mick, that's complicated," he finally said, though that was not even close to an answer.

"Explain it to me; we have time." I knew the drive to Detroit was over an hour.

Ex-Dad drove a little faster, cutting in and out of lanes, but the thing chasing him was in the car and in the past, not in the rearview mirror.

"When you get married, you'll understand," ex-Dad said in that "we're done" tone.

"How?"

"How what?" The words were followed with a loud sigh set at volume ten.

"How will I understand then? I need to understand it now," I said, careful in my words; this wasn't about wanting, for I knew I no longer wanted anything. Anything in the past I had said I wanted—Nicole or Whitney—seemed trivial and childish. This was about need. "Just tell me."

Ex-Dad took a deep breath, no doubt wishing Ford Field was closer to Swartz Creek.

"I'm waiting," I said. My heart was almost exploding with the honesty of the statement.

"Listen, Mick, I don't want to say anything bad about your mother to you," ex-Dad said and I tried not to laugh. I wished I could turn the rearview mirror into a time machine, taking us back into the past so ex-Dad could recall all the bad things he had said to me over the years. To recall all the tears Mom had cried, all the words ex-Dad had yelled, and all the lies he was trying so hard to forget.

"It's not about her," I said, speaking deep from within.

"Marriage is difficult. It's just not for everyone." Ex-Dad's voice lacked the confidence of moments earlier. Obviously examining and accepting responsibility for the mistakes in your life was harder than dissecting special teams.

"For better or worse," I mumbled. I'd seen enough TV to know the words.

"I know the damn wedding vows, Mick."

"You promised."

"Like I said, when you're older, then you'll understand," his voice was slowing down even as the speed of the car increased. We were going about eighty miles an hour yet were still being passed by other cars. I had to wonder what conversations or memories those drivers were running from.

"But why did you cheat?" I asked. I sounded both wise and innocent at the same time. "I mean, how could you do that to Mom? How could you lie to her like that? How could—"

"That's enough, mister!" ex-Dad shouted. He called me "mister" when he was most angry, when he treated me most like a child. It was his human way of lifting his leg.

"No, that's not enough!" I shouted back even if I knew I'd never crack his wall of denial. All I wanted and needed was for him to say, *Mick, what I did was wrong. I'm sorry, forgive me.*

"Can't a guy spend time with his son without this bullshit?" Another shout, another sigh.

"It's not bullshit," I said.

"Watch your mouth, mister," he snapped back.

"But you said it."

"I'm an adult, different rules," ex-Dad proclaimed.

"But why can't I talk like—"

"That's your trouble, you talk too much." Seething had replaced his sighing.

I wanted to ask what he meant, but we both knew. It was something we didn't speak about, but it was always hovering over us like the darkest cloud in a stormy sky. There was never a time I was with him that I didn't remember our conversation after I saw him with that other woman.

The rest of the drive was swallowed in silence. At the game, there were thousands of people in the stands and I wished I could have exchanged seats with any of them. Ex-Dad tried talking to me about the game, but I mostly grunted, shrugged, and gave him nothing in return. Instead, I drifted into dreams. Dreams of running out onto the field and saying, *My name is Mick Salisbury. I'm fifteen years old, and I've helped kill a man. But it's not my fault.*

Nothing is my fault or responsibility. I learned that lesson from my dad. But I also dreamed of saying, *Dad, I'm in big trouble. I need your help.* But deep down, unlike Mom who would risk anything to protect me, I knew ex-Dad would sacrifice nothing. Three hours later, the gun sounded and the Lions ran off the field. A cheer emerged from the stands, but I was quiet.

On the trip home, we talked more about nothing that mattered because for me nothing really did. I wondered if Brody and Aaron felt this way, like having an itch you can't scratch or can't even locate. My heart under my shirt thumped like a rap bass line.

As we pulled off the interstate, ex-Dad didn't drive home but parked us outside of the abandoned GM factory that sat mostly deserted. Ex-Dad shifted in his seat to face me, but I turned away. My eyes were focused on the floor.

"Your mother tells me your grades are starting to slip. Is that true?" ex-Dad asked.

"I guess," I mumbled as I awaited another sigh-filled lecture without him listening to me.

"You have to get your grades up."

"Why?" Out the window, I noticed the darkness of the ghost factory looming larger.

"That's why," ex-Dad said, his voice hoarse from cheering. I looked over to see him pointing out the window. "GM is dying. I don't know how much longer I'll have a job."

"What do you mean?"

"I wonder how things would have been for you if I would have lost my job, like Brody's dad did all those years ago," ex-Dad continued. "I had a little more seniority, so when they drew the line, I stayed on, and Brody's dad fell off. Once he lost his job, I knew that was the beginning of the end for him. It was only a matter of time. That accident was a blessing."

I answered in silence. I thought about saying, *Dad, don't you know that it wasn't an accident? Brody's dad killed himself.* I wondered if I should say, *Dad, do you want to know a secret?* I could tell him something so he would have to reply in return, and answer my question he'd avoided earlier. I was torn between wanting to bond with my father and the bond of my word to Brody. The rubber band I had become was being pulled by both sides. Sooner rather than later, that rubber band would snap, crackle, and then pop.

"I wonder sometimes what would have happened if I'd lost my job then," he said. "In some ways, Brody's dad was the lucky one."

"Lucky?" Was death better than a terrible life? If it was, then didn't we do a good thing putting the Scarecrow out of his misery? Maybe it wasn't murder; it was a mercy killing.

"He had a chance to get out while he was younger," ex-Dad said, then sighed. "He could have started over, but I stayed. I stayed and now I'm the one who's trapped."

I stared at the broken parking lot of the phantom factory. "Trapped?"

"I don't want that for you, Mick, so you've got to work harder. You've got to learn. You've got to think about your future," my father said. "Trouble is, my generation used up most of it."

"I'll try to do better at school." It was the closest I'd felt to my father in some time. It was the most he'd ever revealed to me about himself. I wondered if I would ever experience that again. We drove the rest of the way in silence, neither of us wanting to ruin the moment. At the top of my street, I said, "Dad, I'm sorry about this morning."

Ex-Dad looked at me, puzzled. I wanted to go on and say, *Dad, are you sorry? Not just for this morning, but for everything.* Or, *If you can't say you're sorry, then at least admit the sin. Are you ready?* He didn't apologize or confess, just made more empty promises: "I'll make everything up to you."

"Sure thing," I said as I studied the floor of the car. I didn't believe his words, or mine.

"What the hell!" ex-Dad said out of nowhere. I felt the car speed up as my head jerked up to stare out the windshield at the police car sitting in my driveway.

As we drove toward the house, my mind raced through my choices. The Tahoe was going slow enough, I could jump out and take off running down the street, which would connect to another street, then another, and one of the roads might allow me to escape. Maybe I could turn toward my father and admit it all. *Dad, something happened nine days ago. We'd been drinking, and things got out of hand. It was my fault. You see, I spilled the bottle, and I was the one who mentioned the Scarecrow. Aaron started it, or maybe it was Brody, but it all connects back to me.* Or I could turn toward him and admit nothing, saying instead, *Look, Aaron and Brody, they went crazy and killed this guy. I didn't do anything, I tried to stop them. I wanted to tell. But I have to stand by my friends. That's what you want, right, Dad?* Or I could turn toward him but not turn on my friends: *Dad, I did it. I'm willing to take the consequences. No, nobody else was involved. I'll take the punishment. I'm not afraid of anything anymore.* But I didn't say or do anything; it was like I was paralyzed. When Dad pulled the SUV into the driveway, Mom came to the car with the police at her side.

"Mick, get out of the car please," a black cop said, pointing his finger at me.

As I got out of the SUV, I thought how this must be what a car accident is like: everything happening so fast, and yet you can see everything, take in every detail. I noticed a mole on the white cop's neck and a small scar on the forehead of the black cop. I smelled the Kool smoke surrounding my mother, tasted the donuts from that morning on the back of my teeth, and felt the moisture of the sweat coming from my father's forehead. And I heard every vowel sound of every syllable of every word the white cop spoke when he said, "Michael Salisbury, you're under arrest for the murder of Edward Shreve."

. . .

All the way to the police station, I didn't speak a word. I just sat in the back of the car. I kept my head down and tried not to look into the rearview mirror at ex-Dad's SUV trailing behind us. Mom had stayed behind with cops who were searching the house. My eyes searched the car's floor for a sharp object, not to cut my handcuffed wrists, but to sever my vocal cords.

From the police car, everything happened just like I'd seen on TV: photos, fingerprinting, body searches. From the booking office, I went not to jail but to a holding cell in the courthouse. The room was purgatory: not heaven, not hell, just a place to await my fate. Finally, the door opened and I was taken to another room. There my parents were standing with a guy in a suit whom I didn't know. My parents played their roles perfectly: Mom was worried; ex-Dad was angry.

"Michael, my name is David Richards. The court's appointed me to represent you in this matter." The guy stuck out his hand, but I couldn't move a muscle for fear that one muscle could move another and then another, and then my mouth would move. I did not speak or shake.

"In a little while, you're going to go before a judge," Richards said. "You're going to be charged with the murder of Mr. Shreve. This is a serious offense. Mick, do you understand that? They have just enough evidence to arrest you, maybe even to hold you, but not to convict."

I didn't even blink until Richards looked away and asked my parents to leave us alone.

"You've got to tell me what happened," Richards said, gesturing for me to sit at the table as he sat down next to me. "I can't defend you unless I know what happened. Tell me who this man is, what your connection to him is, and what you did. I need to know the whole story."

I nodded, then cracked my knuckles, but said nothing.

"Mick, this isn't the trial. It's only an arraignment, but it's important. It will determine if you go free today, or if you'll be detained until the next hearing. So, you've got to talk to me."

Nothing.

"I'm going to plead you not guilty," he said. "I've briefly talked to the DA and with what they have, I don't know how they got this far even to arrest you, but the system doesn't work in your favor. I'm going to try to get the charges dropped at this hearing. If not, they can hold you for a few days while we argue that if the case goes on, it should be tried in juvenile court."

My eyes must have given away that I felt like he was speaking some other language.

"All they can do right now is place you with the victim. They arrested you on that, but mainly to get your fingerprints and match them with some evidence at the scene," Richards said.

"What evidence?" I finally broke my silence.

"A lighter. Do you own a lighter, Mick? Bone colored?" he asked.

I could lie, but I knew from watching TV shows that once you got caught in lies, you were toast. The lawyer said he was on my side, but the only thing on my side was my silence.

"I had a lighter. I lost it."

"Okay, how did it get next to the dead man?" Richards asked.

I shrugged.

"Mick, if I'm going to defend you, you need to be honest with me."

"I don't know, okay?" I said, then crossed my arms.

"They also think they have a murder weapon, a brick found near the body," Richards said. I closed my eyes so I wouldn't give away anything. Maybe an eyelash flutter, but nothing else.

"Will they find your fingerprints there?" Richards asked me, to no response. "You need to tell me right now about what happened on that night. I'm not saying you have to talk to the cops, not yet, anyway, but I'm going to tell your parents they need to get a new lawyer if I can't get some co-operation from you. Mick, this is your last chance to let me help you save yourself."

"Go ahead." I could barely talk: all my energy was focused on not speaking.

"Don't do this to yourself or your family," Richards said as he rose from the table. He adjusted his dark blue tie, ran his fingers through his black, gelled hair, and then leaned into me.

I stared at the floor, looking for cracks in the concrete.

"Last chance. You tell me the truth, then I can defend you," Richards said, then bounced his hands off the table. I wanted to tell Richards, but if I told one person, he might tell another. I couldn't afford one crack in the pavement of silence: one crack leads to another, then another.

"I didn't do anything," I said.

"Listen, Mick, this is the most important thing for you

to know," Richards said, then sat back down. He grabbed me by the shoulders, then forced my chin up to look at him. "There's guilt, there's innocence, and there's what they can prove. That's all I care about: what they can prove. They have their version of the truth. I need your version of it so I can defend you."

My head was spinning in fifty directions by Richards's words smashing against my promise to Aaron, to Brody, but mostly to myself. "I've got nothing to say," I mumbled.

"Fine, I'll tell your father. He won't be happy," he said as he left the room.

I wanted to say, *Like I care*, but I let it go. I sat alone in the room for a few moments, cracking my knuckles, looking at the ugly gray walls that seemed to be inching closer.

"Mister, you knock this off right now!" ex-Dad shouted. The door was not shut behind him by the time the sentence was finished. "You'd better start talking, right now, or else."

"Or else what?" I looked down at the table, but felt like I was standing on it. I wanted to say, *How does it feel to want something and not be able to get it? I've wanted you to be there for me, to be a father, but you wouldn't do it, you self-ish bastard. Now, you want something from me. All my life you've had it over me, now I've finally got something over you. I've got my secret.*

"What did you say to me?" He was right in my face. The bulging veins of his neck seemed to be touching the tiny, weak yet growing, hairs on my chin.

"Or else what?" I repeated. "There's nothing you can do to me."

"This is serious, Mick, very serious."

"You can't hit me, you can't ground me, and you can't leave me," I proclaimed.

"I should let you rot in here," he shot back. "I'm trying to help you, son."

Try harder, I wanted to reply, maybe shout, but instead, he pulled out the chair across from me. The scraping of the chair legs on the floor sounded like paper being torn.

"Mick, how did this happen?" His voice was softer now.

"I don't want to—"

"No, not that, this, between us." Ex-Dad sounded lost. "Why are you so angry at me?"

I wanted to shout, *The fact that you have to ask me is all the answer you should need!*

"I'll make you a deal, Mick."

"What?"

"I'll tell you what you want to hear—what we talked about this afternoon—if you tell me what happened. You don't have to tell the lawyer, the cops, or even your mother. It will be a secret just between us," he said.

"Between us?"

"I'm sorry, Mick." Ex-Dad spoke like a first-grader stumbling over a new vocabulary word. "I'm sorry I haven't been a better father. But most of all . . ."

My father let it dangle in the airless room for just a moment.

"I'm sorry I didn't tell you this sooner," he continued, as his words bounced off each other but failed to hit the target of responsibility. "It's hard for me to admit it, to face it."

"Why did you do it?" I asked, knowing I didn't need to explain the pronoun.

"Because, because, Mick, I was selfish. There, I said it, are you happy?"

"Why?"

"Why was I selfish?" Ex-Dad seemed confused. "I don't know, I can't explain."

"I know," I mumbled through the smile I was trying to cover up.

"How do you know?" ex-Dad said.

I was thinking about Brody's and Aaron's dads as well. "Because you were weak," I said, sighed, then put my head facedown on the table. I pretended to hear the molecules of the wood bouncing against each other rather than ex-Dad's grinding teeth and choked-back sighs. I didn't have a watch and there was no clock in the room, but I guessed it was ten minutes before he spoke again.

"Okay, son, now it's your turn," ex-Dad said, each word measured like a precious metal.

I chewed my tongue as the different versions of events flashed like lightning behind my eyes.

"Mick, be a man, keep your promise," Ex-Dad said, but I wanted him to add, *Mick, be a better man than me and keep your promise.*

"Okay, but, Dad, this is between us, right?" Ex-Dad extended his hand and I shook it. "We decided not to go to the football game. We were hanging around the Big K. This homeless guy was bothering us. He asked me for a light, and I handed him my lighter. He ran off with it."

"So you had nothing to do with this?" Ex-Dad spoke the question as a statement of fact.

I nodded with closed and hidden eyes, then asked, "Do you have to tell the lawyer?"

"I'm going to tell him only that you told me you're innocent and that should be enough for him." Ex-Dad had a proud sound in his voice that I'd never really heard before.

"Okay, just tell him I'm innocent. This is just a mistake," I said, still without making eye contact.

"A mistake." Ex-Dad repeated the magic words and then opened the door to leave.

After a few minutes, the lawyer came back into the room and spoke. "It's time."

A cop entered the room. Like kids in costumes marching down the street on Halloween, my lawyer, my parents, the cop, and I walked down a beige hall toward the courtroom. When the courtroom door opened, my senses slowed down again to take it all in. I stared at Aaron and Brody, who were already seated, along with men I guessed were their lawyers, before the white-haired judge. I wasn't given a chance to say anything to Brody and Aaron, but as our lawyers entered our not-guilty pleas, we looked at each other, then nodded. As we were led out, I stared at Brody and at Aaron; I knew no matter what—come hell or high water—none of us would be the first to talk.

Part Three
Thursday, November 18

What would you do?

If I tell on my friends, then I won't go to prison, but how could I live with myself? Your friends are all you have, especially when your family has let you down. They don't lecture you or judge you or ground you or make you feel bad like your parents or teachers do. They're your escape from all that. If you don't have friends, then you don't have any escape. But if I don't tell, then maybe I will go to prison, another place without escape. If none of us tells, maybe we'll all go free; if one of us tells, then that one goes free and the others stay behind bars. I don't know what Brody is saying, what Aaron is saying. I don't know what they're going to do, so how can I know what to do? What would you do?

9:00 a.m.

"It's really simple, kid," the investigator barks at me from across the table. He's trying to scare me. "The one who talks is the one who walks. So, I'll ask you the same thing I did when you came in here four days ago. What happened on November fifth?"

I'm trapped in an impossible situation. He's asking questions but I've got no answers I can give—yet there's so much I want to say. My mind is a mess, littered with fear of the future, thoughts of the past, and one nagging question: how did my fifteen years of life lead me to staring death—in the form of a bloody dead body—in the face?

The investigator stares me down, not even acknowledging Richards sitting next to me in the tiny interrogation room: three walls of stone; one of reflecting glass. "Someone will talk, Mick. Why not make it you?" the investigator says very slowly.

I answer him with an open-mouthed yawn. I can see myself in the mirror, yawning; I know it's one of those two-way jobs. I've seen enough TV cop shows to know that the police and prosecutors can listen in when they're talking to me, but they're not allowed to listen in when I talk to my lawyer or parents—not that I plan to tell them anything, either. The mirror won't open; the wall won't crack; the stone won't bleed.

I'm fighting to stay awake; sleeping on the hard bed and

harder dreams of Genesee County Juvenile Detention Center hasn't been easy for me. I doubt it's easy for Brody or Aaron, either, but I don't know. We're kept separated at the facility, and if my parents are speaking to either Brody's or Aaron's mother, they're not passing on any information. I'm feeling isolated, abandoned, and scared. I've become the Scarecrow.

"Tomorrow, the three of you are going back to court. The judge is going to hear our evidence, and then he's going to decide to try you as an adult. That means hard time, Mick, real hard time. Is that what you want? To spend maybe the rest of your life in prison? You've had a taste of it the last few days. Is that what you want?" The investigator is talking louder now.

I close my eyes, grit my teeth, and start singing "Stairway to Heaven" in my head. I'm not looking at this police officer; I'm just thinking things over one more time.

"You've got the key to let you go. You tell me what I want to know, you tell me what Brody and Aaron did, and why they did it, and you'll go free. Freedom or prison, you decide." The investigator says it like somebody trying to sell me something. The investigator looks to be about the same age as ex-Dad, a little taller, a little less hair, a little fatter, and a lot friendlier smile. Another cop is outside the interrogation room talking with my parents. At least that's what I've been told. My parents wanted to be in the room with me, but I refused. I not only don't want them in the room, I don't want them in the building. I wish my mom wasn't my mom so she wouldn't have to live through this, but I'm glad ex-Dad is feeling pain in *his* guts for once.

"Can they hear us?" I ask Richards as I point to the glass wall.

The investigator jumps in. "It's just a flip of a switch."

I cross my arms like a man who's been gut shot and vow to say nothing else.

"We can put you there. We found your lighter, your prints. We can put Aaron there. We have a blood match. But Brody, we don't have anything on him. My guess is that he's going to talk. Once he talks, he walks, and you'll spend the rest of your life in prison."

My face turns almost as gray as the county-issue shirt and pants.

"I understand the three of you are friends, Mick, but let me tell you something I've learned. It's all about survival. Everybody—you, me, your lawyer, your friends—when it comes right down to it, our urge to survive is the strongest motivator. Brody knows that; he'll talk, you can trust me on that." The investigator is trying to stare me down, but I keep singing in my head.

"Don't listen to him, Mick," my lawyer finally chimes in. I thought he was asleep.

"I hear you're good in math," the investigator says, and it makes me wonder. How does he know that? How does he know anything about me? And if he knows something, then maybe he knows everything. I'm like a frog on the dissection table.

When I don't answer, the investigator stands. Unlike my

teachers' endless droning lectures, I strain to hear every word, while making sure my face and tongue remain frozen as he says, "By the end of the day, we're going to close this case. We've got everything we need for tomorrow's hearing, but I don't think you want that, Mick, do you? When it goes to trial—notice I said *when*, not *if*—and when you are convicted, you'll probably spend the rest of your life in prison. Is that what you want, Mick? I can't imagine how this is going to make your parents feel. Do you really want to put them through that? Maybe somehow you've conned yourself into believing killing Shreve was an accident, so you live with that guilt. But how can you live with the guilt of how your parents are going to feel about their son being in prison? I can help you change all that, right now." The investigator is more preacher than teacher now.

I squirm in my chair at the thought of acting like a snake or a rat. Richards is just listening.

"Don't you want to go home for Thanksgiving?" the investigator asks.

I merely shrug.

"You see, the shit's hitting the fan. The public is outraged. All those bleeding hearts for the poor and the homeless want you convicted. The family of the victim. You see, everybody in the community feels guilty about what happened to a guy like Shreve, how he slipped through the cracks. They didn't do anything to help him when he was alive, so they're going to do it now. There'll be letters to the editors, phone calls to our office, and nobody, Mick, is on your side."

"Interesting information, but you don't have anything on my client," Richards says.

"Read this, Mick." The investigator pulls a newspaper from a file folder. He puts it down in front of me. It's a single page from the *Flint Journal* from Wednesday. I push it away, but he pushes it back at me and I take the bait.

FAMILY OF A HOMELESS MAN EXPRESSES THEIR OUTRAGE

Edward Shreve, 39, was found dead on November 5, in a wooded area behind the WindGate trailer park.

According to law enforcement sources, Shreve was beaten to death and then set on fire, possibly as an attempt to conceal a brutal homicide.

Three Swartz Creek area teenagers are being held at the Genesee County Juvenile Detention Center in connection with the incident. All three are sophomores at Swartz Creek High School; two of them have a violent family history. <See story page 1C>

During an interview with the Flint Journal, *Shreve's family expressed outrage at the savageness of the crime. "They can rot in jail for the rest of their lives so they can think about what they did," Shreve's sister Mary Kramer said. "It was so senseless for these kids in the prime of their lives to go messing with someone like my brother, who was really quite helpless. I hope they understand they took a life. They took away a girl's father."*

Shreve was the youngest of four children. His siblings say he had worked at the GM parts division, but was unable to find another job after being laid off.

"My brother wanted to work, but it was hard for him," Kramer said. "Sometime after he lost his job, he started drinking. Things got a lot worse for him after that."

Kramer said soon after her brother's unemployment insurance ran out, he and his wife divorced. Without a job or place to live, and with his alcoholism growing worse, Shreve started panhandling and sleeping in a makeshift home in the woods behind WindGate trailer park.

Homeless advocates estimate the number of homeless, particularly in the Flint suburbs, is growing at a tremendous rate due to high unemployment and a reduction in state services.

While the city of Flint has services and shelters for the homeless, there are fewer resources in suburbs, according to North End Soup Kitchen spokesperson Margaret Edmonds. Edmonds added, "With growing unemployment, the entire county is faced with more homeless. It would be challenging for any community, especially a smaller one like Swartz Creek."

Shreve's ex-wife and teenaged daughter have turned down our request for an interview. Shreve's daughter attends Swartz Creek High School with the

*three suspects. Police do not believe there is any con-
nection between the daughter and the suspects.*

I finish the story, then grind my fingernails into the bottom of the table.

"You see what I mean?" the investigator says, leaning
into me again. "Everybody is against you, Mick. I'm the only
one on your side. I want to help you, but you need to talk."

"Mick, don't believe him. I'm on your side, he isn't,"
Richards says. The investigator puts the newspaper back
in the folder, a folder that looks to be stuffed full. I wonder
what else is in there and what else has been in the newspaper. What's the story on page 1C?

"I know he's not going to put his family through this. I
know he can see what I see, his mom going to work. Where
does she work, Mick?"

I crack my knuckles again, although not all of them pop.

The investigator quickly glances at his notebook.
"That's right, Chico's. That's a fancy store in the mall, right?
Is that what you want? Your mother going to work and hav-
ing her co-workers and maybe even customers whisper,
'Have you heard about Linda Salisbury's son, Mick?' How
can you put your own mother through an ordeal like that?"

"Shut up!" I shout, then grab hold of the edge of the table.

"At least you're talking now, that's a good start," the investigator says. "But my guess is even by now—what, we've
been in here less than half an hour—Brody's given you up,
probably Aaron as well. I'm willing to hear your side, Mick.
Keep talking, just keep talking."

I so want to say *fuck you*, but I say nothing. But even more, I want to know what's going on in the other rooms. Is Brody talking? Is Aaron? Can I really trust them with my life?

"Remember those floods in New Orleans?" The investigator is standing next to me. "All that started with a crack in the levees. Do you know what a levee is, Mick?"

More failed knuckle cracking on my part.

"A levee holds back water. People trust it works, just like you trust your friends. But when the pressure starts to build, no matter how strong the levee—or how strong a friendship—cracks happen. It takes just one crack. No matter how strong a levee is, all it takes is one crack; once it cracks here, it cracks there, then there, and before you know it, you're drowning. While you're acting tough, in those other rooms it's a different story. Can you hear it?"

But I can't hear anything except "Stairway to Heaven" on replay in my head.

"Can you hear it?" The investigator repeats, then he makes a show of cracking his knuckles. "The levee is breaking. Your friends are telling us that it was all your doing. They're saying that you bashed the guy's head in, stomped in his rib cage, and set him on fire. Once they're done talking, they're going home. They'll sleep in their beds, while you'll be in a cell—but not in a place like this. You'll do time in the state prison full of murderers and rapists."

"Stop trying to scare him—" Richards starts to say.

"I'm trying to save you, Mick. You're about to go under. I'm reaching out a hand to help you, and you're going to turn that away? You're drowning and I'm offering to save your life. The water is rising, Mick," the investigator says, reaching his hand across the table, but I turn away.

"A picture is worth a thousand words, right?" the investigator says, then opens up the folder again. He pulls out some photographs, then pushes one across the table at me.

I quickly look at the photo, then wonder if the cop can hear my heart beating, or can sense my soul leaving my body.

"What we have here, Mick, is a photo of the three of you outside the Big K Market on Friday, November fifth. It's from the video camera outside. It seems to me you're having a good time," the investigator says, almost smiling as he taps the photo with his index finger. "You see the time stamp there on this image we've lifted from their outside camera? Do you see it, Mick?"

I stare at my own smiling face in the grainy black-and-white photos. I flash on that night and wonder how I could have thought anything was funny; I stare at the tiled walls around me now and wonder if anything will ever be funny again.

"We compared the time you were outside the Big K with the time that Mr. Shreve was inside. Guess what, Mick, it is the exact same time," the investigator says, then leans into me.

"All circumstantial," Richards says. The investigator takes more photos from the folder, putting them down quickly in front of me, like he was dealing blackjack. These color photos show the remains of a human being with burned skin hanging off of broken white bone.

"Here are photos of what was left of Shreve," the investigator says, pushing the photos toward me. I stare at them as if I was seeing an accident on the side of the road. "Mick, look at these photos."

"This is wrong—" Richards starts, but the cop cuts him off.

"We can do this the hard way or the easy way," the investigator says.

I try to resist, but I can't, so I ask, "What do you mean?"

"Easy way is simple: Mick, tell us what happened. I admire your loyalty to your friends. You'd only better hope and pray they are as loyal to you. My guess is they're not as loyal and they'll save themselves. Hard way is we go to trial and everybody sees these photos. Which is it going to be for you?" The investigator flipped his friendly smile switch. Now he's all teeth.

"Don't answer that," Richards says.

"I'm guessing that Mick probably got caught up in something that his friends did. If he turns on Brody and Aaron, and we believe him, then we'll recommend the case to juvenile court," the investigator says. "No prison time, for sure. Detox or some program if drugs or alcohol were involved. Probation, community service, and maybe some sort of restitution."

"I see," Richards says, but I don't like the interested tone in his voice.

"Christmas is coming up and this is a gift," the investigator says with a smile. "But we're closing this out. Brody may seem tough, but he's ready to talk, I can tell. And the other one, Aaron, he knows the system, so he knows if he talks, then he'll get the walk."

I avert my eyes from the drowning-pool blues of the investigator.

"Aaron seems the weak link," the investigator says to Richards. "From what happened to his dad, he knows that it's better if you don't have to stand in front of a jury. Aaron will sell you out to save himself hard time like his father's doing. You really want him to decide your fate?"

I can't take much more; it's like there's a ticking time bomb in my chest.

"Brody's a Catholic, right?" the investigator asks, but doesn't wait for an answer. "Well, they say confession is good for the soul. It might start with confessing his sins to a priest, but that won't be enough. Brody will talk to us. He'll tell us everything. Maybe he'll tell us this was all Mick's fault. Is that what he'll say, Mick? I want you to connect the dots. There is a dead man and you're involved. We know that. Someone is going to go to prison for that crime. We know that. What we don't know is who that person should be: you, Brody, or Aaron. Three people know who did what: you, Brody, and Aaron. The first to talk is the one who walks."

"We're done now," Richards cuts him off. The investigator nods, then opens up the folder.

"While you're thinking about things, you might want to read this," the investigator says just before he exits. "It might explain why we're more willing to believe you than your friends."

TWO TEENAGERS ACCUSED IN BEATING OF HOMELESS MAN HAVE VIOLENT FAMILY HISTORY

Two of three teenagers being held for the murder of Edward Shreve, a homeless man, have a violent family history.

One has a father who is currently on death row at Huntsville State Prison in Texas for the brutal murder of his son.

Another's family also has a violent background. One brother is currently serving a ten-year sentence at Leavenworth Military Prison in Leavenworth, Kansas, for assaulting an officer. The same suspect was recently removed from a school activity for violating the school's code of conduct for students.

Investigators have learned that earlier in the day, this suspect had an altercation at the Space Invaders arcade with a student from Flushing High School.

The third teenager has no history of violence.

Police have yet to learn how the paths of the three teenagers and Shreve crossed on the night of November 5. Police also lack a motive for the killing.

I read the story twice, slower the second time, hoping the words would change. I stall for time, taking a drink of water, but it does nothing to squelch the burning in my stomach. I notice the investigator left the photos of the Scarecrow faceup inches away from me.

"Mick, what do you want to do here?" Richards asks, then turns over the photos.

"Just leave me alone," I say.

"Look, I'm not going to pressure you like the cop. I want what is best for you, but it doesn't look good. I think he's probably right about Brody and Aaron," Richards says.

"I said leave me alone!" My shout is loud enough to cause the glass of water to vibrate. We sit in silence for a few minutes, although the volume in my head is up to ten. The photos of the burned up Scarecrow are turned over, but I still hear Robert Plant singing. I'm distracted when the investigator re-enters carrying a small brown box. "Mick, your parents want to join us. I know you don't want that, but they get to choose, not you."

My parents walk into the room behind the investigator.I want to scream at them to leave. They're standing behind me: Mom's hand is on my shoulder; ex-Dad is seething like a boiling pot. Mom finally sits, but ex-Dad remains standing, five feet and one hundred miles away.

"So who is Garrett Barber?" the investigator asks, like he was talking about the weather.

"He's this kid—" ex-Dad starts to say.

"Let him speak, Mr. Salisbury, it's really best," the investigator says. "Mick, who is he?"

"A kid at school," I mumble.

"Really?" The investigator furrows his brow. "Mick, we've been finding out a great deal about you since you've been in here. You can sit here and lie to us, but what good is that going to do? We either already know or will find out the truth. So, again, who is Garrett Barber?"

"Tell him," ex-Dad says, slapping his hand hard against the back of my chair.

I don't move a muscle, not even a molecule within a muscle.

"He told us that you and Brody beat him up," the investigator says, then looks at Richards and away from me. "Sounds like your client *does* have a history of violent behavior."

I wanted to turn to Mom and tell her—but only her—why I had a fight with Garrett, that I was defending her. And it was Brody who did the beating up, not me. The investigator pulls a folder from the box, then puts it in front of me next to the Shreve pictures.

"I have his statement right here if any of you would like to look at it." The investigator hands the folder to Richards, who starts to speed read through the pages. When it becomes obvious I won't answer him, the investigator pulls out another folder.

"And who is Nicole Snider?" the investigator continues. "We've talked to her and her father. He was thinking of taking out a restraining order—"

"What the hell is going on?" ex-Dad explodes. I want to say, *That's a lie,* but what is truth and what is lie is confused in my head now. "Why were you stalking this girl?"

"My son isn't a stalker," Mom says. I notice that she says "my son," not "our son," when speaking about me, even with ex-Dad in the room. I feel bad making Mom spend so much time in this room with ex-Dad; her skin must be crawling.

"Again, it's all right here." The investigator hands another folder to Richards. "Mick, do you want to tell your side of the story? Mr. Snider was very convincing and very angry."

This is all wrong. All wrong.

"How about a Natalie Riley?" the investigator says, but I'm confused by this name.

"Who are these girls?" Mom says, not really asking me, just desperate to know.

"Your son, Mrs. Salisbury, made a lewd sexual remark to this young woman at the Space Invaders arcade, which led to—guess what?" the investigator continues in a monotone voice.

I remember the girl and realize the investigator must know everything about me.

"It led to another act of violence with your son and Brody Warren attacking a young man at the arcade," the investigator says. "A jury will be very interested in this pattern of violence. The young man said he would testify at your trial. That is, if you want a trial. Like we've said, you don't need to do that, just tell us what happened that night with Mr. Shreve."

More silence from me; tears from Mom; sighs from ex-Dad. Everything's normal.

"Here's his statement," the investigator says, handing yet another folder over to Richards. "Still don't want to talk, Mick? Fine, let's continue."

As sweat drips from my forehead, I'm beginning to understand the levee analogy.

"So we have these acts of violence, one of them on the day of the attack," the investigator says, then pulls out another folder. "But then we've yet to add in the accelerant to your son's behavior. The same accelerant they used to try to burn the body: alcohol."

"My son doesn't—" Mom rushes in armed with her beliefs about me, not the facts.

"We talked to some students at your school and they said your nickname is 151," the investigator says. I imagine every student at school talking about me, like they once talked about Brody's football heroics. But all the talk is nothing more than a public humiliation. No matter what happens, I know I'll never ever be able to attend Swartz Creek High School again.

"151? What the hell does that mean?" ex-Dad asks, slapping the chair again.

"Why don't you tell your father about your nickname?" The investigator is smiling again, but not the friendly smile. No, this is the smile of a willing and well-paid executioner.

"You'd better start talking, mister!" Another shout from ex-Dad, another slap.

"No?" The investigator shrugs. "151 stands for Bacardi 151 Rum, isn't that right, Mick?"

"That is irrelevant," Richards says, trying to ignore, as I am, Mom's tears.

"I've got someone who will testify about Mick's impaired judgment when intoxicated." The investigator pulls out another folder. He taps on the table waiting for me to speak.

When I give him nothing but a cold stare, he says, "If you don't want to talk about Garrett Barber or Nicole Snider or Natalie Riley, then how about Roxanne Gray?"

"Shut up!" I shout; I can't take it anymore. I'm almost ready to talk to make this stop, so Mom doesn't have to hear any more about the secret and shameful life I've been hiding from her.

"Calm down, Mick," Richards says. "He's trying to upset you, rattle you."

The investigator offers the folder to Mom, saying, "A drunken sexual incident at a party."

"Stop this," Mom pleads.

"Linda, be quiet!" ex-Dad shouts from across the room.

"I know it must be hard, Mrs. Salisbury, I got two kids of my own." The investigator's rough voice has grown smooth, like he pulled a switch. "You try to raise them right, teach them good values, but they get away from you. It's not your fault, don't blame yourself for what your son has become. Bad influence of these other two has made your son become a murderer."

"My son hasn't become anything," Mom cuts in. "He's a good child and—"

The investigator cuts her off, saying, "A child doesn't have this history of violent behavior. A child doesn't perform sex acts. And a child doesn't watch movies like this."

The investigator pulls from the box the *Filthy First Times* DVD and my death is total.

"Oh, Mick," Mom says, then turns to leave the room. I wait for my father to say "That's mine," but the only sound in the room is Mom's footsteps, not ex-Dad's admission. Same old shit.

"I've had enough," ex-Dad announces, then walks over to me. He grabs my chin and yanks my face around so I have to look at him. "What happened to you? I raised you better, mister!" My eyes look down, but I want to raise my voice and shout, *You never raised me. You chased women, then left me and Mom. You're not my responsible father, you're just my sperm donor.*

"So, there you have it, Counselor," the investigator says. "And this was just a few days of investigating. Mick, what else are we going to find? Can you really risk that? No judge or jury is going to buy the innocent act. Mick, you're guilty and *everyone* in this room knows it."

"We're done," Richards announces, slapping his hands on the table.

"I'll leave this all with you, Counselor," the investigator says. "You can tell your client how we'll bring this all out when he goes to court. Everybody is going to know every-thing about you. *Every* little *detail.*"

"I don't think so," Richards replies.

"And then we'll have the photos of the man that your client brutally murdered," the investigator says, standing up, taking his Pandora's box with him. "It's about the weight of the evidence. Mick, do you feel the weight of all of this on top of you? Do you feel it? Just tell me what happened and all of this goes up in smoke."

He demonstrates the final phrase by taking from the box my lighter sealed in an evidence bag. "Your lighter, your prints, your history. We've got one dead body, and you've got two untrustworthy friends. Mick, you're smart. Add it up and know there's only one path to take.

"I'll give you time to think about it," the investigator says. "Mr. Richards, Mr. Salisbury, why don't we talk about this outside? Let's give Mick time to make the right choice."

. . .

Through the glass, I imagine the conversations between ex-Dad and Richards. I imagine my mother's tears. I imagine conversations down the hallway with Brody, his lawyer, that cop, and Brody's mom. I imagine Aaron and that set of conversations. But all I can do is imagine because I can't see through the thick walls. I can't hear what others are saying; I can only imagine. I can only hear what's already been said about me; I can only hear myself saying, *I'm ready to talk.* But even as I practice forming the words, I know I can't turn on my friends for there is nothing worse in the world than cheating on those you love. I've cheated once and paid the price. The police may be dealing from the bottom of the deck, but I want to dig deep and find the best part of myself even in the shadow of my worst deeds. I just want to sleep. I'm exhausted from not sleeping and not telling the truth. I close my eyes, but sleep won't come. After maybe a half hour, the door opens and another cop walks in with Richards.

"Mick, I'm Detective Allan," the man says, then sits down. I grunt, look up, and notice the wide smile on Allan's face. Allan's older, gray-haired, and his voice sounds like he's not going to be surprised by anything. "I've talked to Aaron and Brody. We got the whole story, Mick."

I don't say anything. Richards looks as stunned as I do.

"We've got Aaron's story, and we've got Brody's, so that leaves you," Allan says, pushing a blank sheet of paper across the table. "You're all alone, Mick, all alone."

"What do you mean?"

"They've both given you up," Allan almost whispers, the paper pushed a little closer. "So if you were counting on your friends to protect you, if the three of you had some sort of agreement, if you thought you could trust them—Wrong. Wrong. Wrong."

"I don't believe you," I say, mostly to convince myself.

"Aaron said you were the one who killed Shreve and burned up the body," Allan says, pushing the paper closer. "If you want to tell us something different, then start writing."

I'm weighing the words in my jam-packed skull as Allan looks through his notes.

"Here's what he said, 'Mick was the one who killed the Scarecrow,'" Allan says as the fire alarm goes off between my ears. How did Allan know to use the term 'the Scarecrow'? Did Brody and Aaron really confess? If so, did they both blame me? Or is Allan lying to me? The crack in the levee is getting wider; the first investigator was right. I feel like I'm drowning.

"Brody and Aaron are my friends. They wouldn't say anything," I protest.

"I've seen a lot of folks doing hard time with that attitude,"

Allan says. "If you want to pin your hopes on these two, well, Mick, that is your choice. I'm not your parent, I'm not your lawyer. But I can tell you you're making a mistake. Prisons are full of guys thinking they had friends, but realizing too late that they were friends second, and humans with the urge to save themselves first. Brody cracked right away, but Aaron took longer. They're survivors, Mick."

I don't hear him; I just hear Plant singing. If only I can keep it together.

"Brody acted all tough, but I think when he talked to that girl—" Allan says.

"What girl?" I interject.

"Lauren Shreve, the victim's daughter," Allan says. "She's seen him a couple of times."

"Why wasn't I notified?" Richards says quickly.

"You're not his attorney. Who Mr. Warren sees is between him and his lawyer, but I thought your client might find it interesting that Brody has been talking with her," Allan says, then chuckles, another hook that reels me in. "You just have to wonder what was said, no?"

"What's so funny?" I ask.

"They talked in person rather than over the phone," Allan says, then scans his notes. "What did you guys call her?—that's right, Cell Phone Girl."

Everyone in the room sees it happening at once. The levee's been compromised somewhere. Somebody talked: nobody but the three of us ever called her that name. Allan leans in; he must have sniffed out the fear sweating down my forehead like a raging river.

"Here's a pen, Mick," Allan says, laying the black object on the blank piece of white paper. "Write down what happened if you can't tell us. We can end this today."

"No." I cross my arms. He picks the pen up and clicks it like a stopwatch.

"Mick, to be honest, we're still inclined to believe you, cut you some slack," Allan says.

"What do you mean?" Richards asks.

"Brody, he's just a punk. We see kids like him in the system every day," Allan says. "And Aaron, good kid, but damaged. So, I'm sorry to break the news to you, but your friends rolled on you. You might as well return the favor and roll on them."

I'm singing the end to "Stairway to Heaven" over and over like a stuck CD, the same part of the song repeating endlessly in my head.

"So, we've heard their stories, and we think they're probably lying," Allan says. "But the only way we'll know for sure is if we hear your side. Once we have your version, then we can compare the three, but to be honest, Mick, your story would have the most credibility."

"You'd better listen to this," Richards says.

"Mick, I'm waiting for your answer," Allan says. "Time to tell us the truth."

I want to say, *Answer, here's your answer: fuck you.* There's a faint click of a heater coming on. There's the ticking of Richards's watch and the clicking of Allan's pen. There's the beating of my heart. Outside, I imagine, there is the spilling of Mom's tears.

"Last chance," Allan says, snatching the paper off the table. "If I walk out that door now without your statement, then all we have left is the physical evidence that puts you at the scene, and the signed confessions of Brody and Aaron. We've shown you how we know everything about your life and we'll tell it to the jury. But, if I leave now without your signed confession, then the next time we'll see each other is when the judge sentences you to prison. You're too smart for that, Mick," Allan says.

"Mick, let's—" Richards starts, but I just shake my head violently.

"Bad choice, kid, bad choice," Allan says, then starts toward the door.

"Wait!" I shout just as Allan taps on the glass so he can exit the room.

"You got something to say?" Allan turns, the smile is back, bigger, more inviting.

"I want to talk with my mom," I say softly, hiding my eyes, shame, sorrow, guilt.

Allan doesn't say anything as he closes the door behind him.

"Alone," I say to Richards.

"I'm going to try to talk to your friends' lawyers, see what's really going on," Richards says, then rises from the table. "But, Mick, you have to decide what's best for you, not your friends."

"I know," I admit out loud, more to myself than to Richards.

"Even if Allan's lying about Brody and Aaron confessing, I think he's right that they probably will crack and blame you. Even if one of them gives you up, that's bad for us."

"I know," I mutter, even though I don't know anything for sure anymore.

"I'm going to find out what's going on," Richards says, then walks to the door. As he taps on the glass, he turns to me. "Don't say anything to the police or sign anything until I get back, understand?"

As minutes pass and Mom doesn't come into the room, I wonder if she's deserted me. If so, I couldn't blame her: I'm a screw-up who has brought her nothing but shame and sorrow. My guilt isn't over the Scarecrow, but about scarring my mom's life. She deserves better than my father, better than me, and better than watching her son go to prison. I have to protect her again.

. . .

"Mick, are you ready to talk?" Mom says softly as she finally enters the room a few minutes later. I don't know if I'm strong enough to withstand that look on her face, the one she wears that says, *You are my son, I will love you and protect you no matter what.*

"I don't know," I mumble.

"You don't need to tell the police what happened, because I know you," Mom says.

"Can they hear us?" I ask, then point at the two-way mirror.

"I know that you couldn't have done something like this," Mom says in reply.

"Thanks, Mom."

"And this evidence, I'm sure there's a good reason for all of it," Mom continues.

I don't know whether to smile or cry.

"Do you know why, Mick?" she asks, but doesn't give me a chance to answer. "I know you couldn't have done something this terrible because if you had, I know you would have told me. I know you're a good person, Mick, and I know if you'd done something bad, that you would have to tell someone, and that someone would be me."

Sitting in the tiny room, I wished I could just disappear. "Mom, I'm not perfect."

"I know that, Mick, I guess even more now," she says as images of DVDs, rum bottles, and Roxanne flash through my mind, but no doubt are burned into Mom's memory.

"I'm sorry, Mom, I'm so sorry," I repeat.

I stop talking because I can't lie to her anymore. I stop breathing for a microsecond because I can't imagine her disappointment in me. I stop telling myself that it's not my fault because even if I didn't smash a brick into the Scarecrow's head, there's blood on my hands.

"I know you couldn't live with yourself if you'd done something so terrible." Her voice has a slight tremor. "You couldn't do that to another person. You couldn't do that to me."

"To you?" I say.

"I know you couldn't do something that would hurt me, like going away to prison. It would destroy me to think you did this and then lied to me about it. That's why I believe you. I believe you because you know that if you lied about this, it would destroy me."

I feel like a prisoner falling through the gallows and twisting in the air.

"Mick, look at me." She takes my hands and squeezes them until my knuckles lose color. "I love you more than I could tell you, and if you care about me at all, then you need to tell me and the police exactly what happened, but—"

"But?"

"I know you had more to do with this than you've told us. It's going to hang over you unless you set it free. You've got to accept responsibility and then you'll feel better. Trust me."

"I know, Mom, I know." I can't hold back tears much longer.

"I know you want to protect your friends. I know you want to save yourself. Mick, the worst thing you can do now is lie to me or to the police," Mom continues, "because the truth always comes out. You can make up stuff or cover it up, but the truth always emerges. I know you're confused about what to do and what to say, but if you tell the truth, then you won't feel that way. You won't hurt anymore. You need to start healing."

"I can't," is all I can say: two words to stand for the two thousand I can't say.

"Mick, please don't do this to me, to yourself," she continues. "I told you one day you'd talk to me. That day has to be today."

I take a deep breath, then out comes the contents of my lungs along with the words I've been holding back. I must admit what I am: helpless. "Mom, tell me what to do."

"There's only one thing to do," she replies. "Do the right thing. Tell the truth."

"No matter what?"

"I know it's trite, but it's true. The truth will set you free." She squeezes my hands again, but I stand mute. When I say nothing, she let's go and her face turns cold. "If you don't tell the truth, then—"

"Then what?" I ask. She pauses for seconds that seem like hours before she speaks.

"If you don't tell the truth, then I can't love you anymore, Mick," she finally says.

I want to scream, but no sound will give my pain the justice it deserves.

"I've been lied to too much by your father, and I won't let it happen to me again. If you've lied to me, then I can't love you anymore, Mick. There's no worse punishment these people can give you than that. To know that your own mother, the woman who brought you into this world and raised you, doesn't love you anymore," Mom says.

"Mom, what are you saying?" I ask after recovering from stunned silence.

"Mick, you have a choice to make, probably the biggest choice you'll ever make in your life. You need to choose between your friends and your family. You need to choose between telling the truth or living a lie. You need to choose if you still want to be my son," Mom says, then rises and starts toward the door.

"Wait!" I shout, but when I try to say more, no words come out, only an anguished sound. It is the sound of shame, regret, and guilt. It is the sound of tears, rage, and sorrow.

My mother moves toward the table and sits down across from me. She touches me again, this time lightly on the shoulder like she was pushing the play button on my jPod.

"Here's what really happened—" I start, trying to unravel the truth from the lies. My tongue burns as I speak the truth and nothing but: word for word, minute for minute, blow by blow of what I did, what Aaron did, what Brody did. As I speak, Mom never says a word, although her eyes tear and her mouth drops. She wanted the truth; she should've known better.

When I finish by admitting to burning the body, the life seems to leave my mother's body, just like I saw the Scarecrow's soul rise on November 5.

"I'm so sorry, Mom, I'm so sorry," I confess, my voice thick with tears.

"I know, Mick," she replies softly. "I'm sorry, too."

"I wish I could take it all back," I say, wiping my running nose with the sleeve of the gray shirt. "Things just got out of control, but that's no excuse."

"I always wondered," Mom says after a moment of silence.

"Wondered what?"

"If you were going to turn out like your father, or if you would be a better man," Mom says, but I can't capture the strange emphasis she put on the word *father*.

"What do you mean?"

"If you would accept responsibility, if you would be a man," she says sharply. "This is a horrible thing you've done, but you've admitted to it. You're a better man than your father, and I've finally been able to protect you like a mother should. We're all ready to heal now, Mick."

"Heal?" and the word clicks in my head: everything is connected to something else, but the click is real. It's the sound of the door to the room opening. Both of the cops, as well as my lawyer, come into the small space, which seems even smaller. My father is missing in action.

"You did the right thing," the investigator says, but the comment is meant for Mom, not me. My heart shakes like thunder as lightning hits. I realize Mom didn't answer my question "Can they hear us?" when I pointed to the two-way mirror that the investigators were behind as I confessed every detail of how Brody and Aaron murdered the Scarecrow. My friendship bonds are forever broken with my words; my family triangle complete with Mom's betrayal of me.

TWO TEENAGERS HELD IN BEATING OF HOMELESS MAN TO BE CHARGED WITH SECOND-DEGREE MURDER; OTHER TO FACE LESSER CHARGES

November 19

The Flint Journal *has learned that two of the teens arrested for the murder of a homeless man in Swartz Creek will be arraigned today as adults on charges of second-degree murder. The third teenager in the case will plead to a lesser charge in return for his testimony against the other two. No other details have been released.*